A

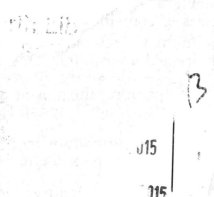

B

015

015

D1392824

LIGHTNING DRAW

He drifted into the Golden Nugget saloon in the ugly township of Come Lucky ... Born in a wild and six-gun-torn West — the Cougar Kid was named after the most vicious animal that roamed the country. He was an ordinary cowpoke, but lawlessness and savagery had turned him into a ruthless killer. And now men like Jumbo Jordan, a rattlesnake of a man who runs a protection racket, will find no mercy when they face the deadly Cougar Kid ...

HANK FISHER

LIGHTNING DRAW

Complete and Unabridged

LINFORD
Leicester

First published in Great Britain in 2008 by
Robert Hale Limited, London

Originally published in paperback as
Cougar Kid by Shaun O'Hara

First Linford Edition
published 2010
by arrangement with
Robert Hale Limited, London

British Library CIP Data

Fisher, Hank.
    Lightning draw.- -(Linford western library)
    1. Western stories.
    2. Large type books.
    I. Title II. Series III. O'Hare, Shaun.
    Cougar Kid.
    823.9'14–dc22

    ISBN 978–1–44480–129–3

11446098

Published by
F. A. Thorpe (Publishing)
Anstey, Leicestershire

Set by Words & Graphics Ltd.
Anstey, Leicestershire
Printed and bound in Great Britain by
T. J. International Ltd., Padstow, Cornwall

This book is printed on acid-free paper

1

He was not known as the Cougar Kid that night he pushed through the swing doors of the Golden Nugget saloon. The name had still to be bestowed on him.

He was just a stranger when he drifted into the small, ugly, sun-bleached township of Come Lucky, a few miles north of the Rio Grande where the vast plains of Texas meet the rockier terrain of New Mexico.

No one knew whom he was or where he had come from. No one bothered to ask. It was the one thing you didn't do in the south-west in those days when men strong enough to keep what they could grab were building up a beef-empire . . . you didn't ask a man about his past. You accepted him for what he was; judged him only as you knew him — and on how fast he could handle a long-barrelled Colt.

He had ridden into town on that big, ungainly black of his, hitched it outside the Golden Nugget, pushed his way inside and ordered a shot of liquor. He was a slim, thin-faced man, with high cheekbones, granite-chip eyes, and a frosty smile when something appealed to his sense of cynicism.

There was a hell of a lot of noise in the saloon that night. Outside, to the north of Come Lucky, a huge herd was in the process of building up ready for the long trek up the Chisholm Trail to the railhead at Dodge City. All the ranches around were chipping in to make one vast herd. The bigger the herd, the better its chance of winning through. And boys from the ranches which had already completed the beef round-up had hit town with up to three months' pay in their pockets — and when a cowhand has dough to burn he's inclined to do it in a hell-raisin', rumbustious way.

The floor of hard-packed earth

echoed to the thud of high-heeled riding boots. The big wooden shell of the building rang with the whoops of cowhands on the spree — and with the shrill, high-pitched artificial laughter of the good-time girls Lew Reardon, who ran the place, had imported from back east. They would have come even without Lew Reardon, of course, for wherever there is big money, there you will find the female gold-miners. You could find them in scores of places like Come Lucky, those here-today-gone-tomorrow shanty-towns that sprang up and died as the beef frontier was pushed further and further west.

The faro table and chuckaluck wheel were going full tilt. Under one of the big kerosene lamps that lit the place, Lew's brother, Jud, had a poker school on the go.

It had taken the boys from the ranches three months of hard, solid graft to earn the money they brought with them into town that night. Long, hard days had gone into earning it

. . . endless hours in the saddle . . . sweat and guts — and the risk of sudden death. Lew and Jud and the good-time girls would take the lot from them in as many hours. No one minded that very much — so long as the liquor was the real stuff, the good-time girls weren't too good, and the gambling games were on the square.

But the poker school was definitely not on the square.

Jud Reardon, with his black jacket, his black string tie and his slim white hands, looked every inch what he was — a tinhorn gambler. He carried the deck of cards around the table in his hands as he dealt, a trick a man uses when he may want to deal from the bottom upon occasions.

The thin-faced stranger over by the bar noted the point as he downed his liquor.

He was dressed like any other cowhand in the Golden Nugget that night — stetson, neckerchief, fancy shirt, buckskin chaps, high-heeled riding boots. He might have been a cowhand — except that he wore twin Colts. One gun was usual — ordinary — matter-of-fact. An essential part of life — if you wanted to go on enjoying it. A cowhand without a gun would have felt undressed, naked. But two!

Two guns stamped a man as being apart from his fellows. They stood for offence — not defence. And when they were carried in cutaway scabbards to make for a quick draw, with the tips of the scabbards lashed down around the thighs, they stamped a man as the type to steer clear of. So the stranger stood alone, drank alone. Even the good-time girls gave him a wide berth. It didn't appear to worry him any.

Nor did the crooked goings-on at the poker table.

He shrugged, turned back to the bar, ordered another rye. It was none of his business. The bartender sent bottle and glass spinning towards him with a practised flip of the fingers. They stopped, side by side, an inch short of the edge. The stranger tossed a quarter on to the bar and poured out.

'I saw that, you dirty cheat.'

The shout rang out loud and clear even above the general hubbub in the saloon. There was a sudden silence around the card table — a silence which crept gradually into the far corners of the big room. It was almost a physical thing, that silence, as real and tangible as the blue haze of cigarette smoke which writhed and crept in the yellow glare of the oil lamps. A girl's laugh broke it, loud, high-pitched, a shade hysterical. The laugh was cut off as clean as though it had been done with a knife, but it turned the silence into a murmur of apprehension, and the swing doors agitated as one or two of the more nervous spirits slipped out into the night.

In the big mirror which ran the whole length of the back of the bar the stranger had a clear view of the tableau at the card table. Two men had half risen from their seats. One was Jud Reardon. The other was Matt Bronson, part-owner of the Crazy Y. They were leaning towards one another, their arms outstretched. Reardon's hands held the deck of cards with which he had been dealing. Bronson's hand was about one of Reardon's wrists.

Reardon's clipped accents were clear and precise.

'You're drunk, Bronson. Let go of my wrist.'

There was no doubt that young Bronson had had about all the liquor he could carry. His cheeks were flushed; his eyes hot and bright. His voice, when he spoke, was a little thick.

'I want my dough back, Reardon. You've been cheating. That card you dealt me came from the bottom of the deck. Didn't it?'

He looked round. The other three men at the card table, shrugged, shuffled their feet, avoided his gaze.

You thought twice before you accused

a man of cheating at cards in Texas. Even if you could prove your point, you still thought twice — unless you were mighty handy with a Colt. For old man Colt was more often than not the sole arbiter — judge, jury, and executioner rolled into one. And most certainly you thought twice before you accused Jud Reardon of cheating. To accuse Jud meant a reckoning with Lew.

The sudden silence brought Lew to the door labelled 'Office' in crude white lettering.

He stood there, a big bull of a man, thick-necked, heavy-browed, his bulk taking up most of the space of the narrow doorway. The backs of his hands were a mass of black hairs. The hands were rock-steady, the thumbs crooked over the hammers of the six-guns they held.

'Who says the games in the Nugget are crooked?' he demanded.

The space between the doorway and the card table cleared as if by magic.

It was a scene the Golden Nugget

had witnessed many times before.

Matt Bronson let go of Jud's wrist and straightened up. His chair went over with a clatter as he did so. He seemed to sway a little on his feet.

His tongue came out and licked dry, cracked lips. Knowledge of what he had let himself in for was beginning to penetrate through the haze of liquor which fogged his brain.

'I — he — Jud dealt me from the bottom of the deck,' he mumbled.

Reardon came clear of the doorway, crouching a little. With a deliberate motion he thrust his guns back into their holsters. Behind him, in the office, Lila, the slim dark Mexican girl he lived with, showed her white teeth in a quick smile. She knew what was coming. So did everyone else in the Nugget.

Reardon said: 'Go for your gun, Bronson.'

Matt Bronson looked down at the gun slung at his right thigh; looked up again at the big, beefy figure of Reardon. There seemed to be two

Reardons — swaying, meeting, merging. Quite suddenly, Bronson realized that he was drunk. Too drunk to stand even a halfway chance with Reardon.

'You heard me, Bronson. Go for your gun or do I shoot you down where you stand?'

From the shadows at the back of the room a voice said: 'He's drunk, Reardon. You can see that. Leave him alone.'

Reardon's eyes swept the crowd of faces.

'Keep out of this,' he said. 'This is between me and Bronson. Well, Bronson?'

Matt Bronson passed a hand across his eyes; shook his head dazedly.

'I — I'm no match for you, Reardon.'

There was a sudden murmur from around the room. Everyone knew what it must have cost him to say that; to back down in the face of gunplay.

Reardon laughed.

'Too darned true, Bronson. Drunk or sober, you're no match for Lew

Reardon.' His hands moved and swept up again with guns in them. 'You've got a lot to learn, Bronson, so get started. Down on your knees now and apologise to Jud.'

Under his neat moustache Jud's teeth showed in an ugly grin. Lila, the Mexican girl, drifted into the doorway behind Lew to watch the sport. She leaned negligently against the doorpost, one hand caressing her dark hair.

'Hurry it up, Bronson. Down now. On both knees. Tell Jud how sorry you are for speaking such lies about him.'

A cowpuncher sniggered. Bronson meant nothing to him, and this sort of devilment was just good clean fun to men leading the tough, lusty life which the vast, open beef-empire of Texas demanded.

'But it wasn't a lie, Reardon.'

Heads pivoted as though jerked by strings. It was the stranger over by the bar who had spoken. Reardon's gaze swept in the direction of the stranger. 'Who says it wasn't?'

11

'I do, Reardon.'

The crowd in the saloon hastily rearranged itself to leave another clear avenue between Reardon and the stranger. The stranger wasn't even looking at Reardon as he spoke. He was still leaning on the bar, looking into the mirror behind it. He drained his glass, straightened up, turned, walked slowly towards Reardon.

He was quite young — little more than a kid. Until you looked at his eyes. Then you realized that he was no kid. They were eyes that had been around; seen a lot of things in the time they'd been around.

At the back of the crowd someone whispered to his neighbour: 'Who's the kid?'

The other shook his head.

'Dunno. Stranger to these parts. Never seen him in Come Lucky afore.'

'His holsters are lashed down.'

'They'll need to be if he's gonna tangle with Reardon.'

Reardon evidently thought so, too.

He gave a big snort of derision.

'Well, well. Another young rooster with too much crow. You drunk, too?'

The stranger shook his head. 'No, Reardon, I'm not drunk.' His voice, it was noticeable, lacked the usual drawl of the home-reared Texan. His face was strictly deadpan; absolutely without expression of any sort. His hands were in front of him, chest high, one set of fingers lazily scratching the backs of the other — a gesture which was later to become known far and wide throughout that triangular beef empire which had its base along the Rio Grande and its apex in Dodge City. 'Your brother was dealing from the bottom of the deck. Not just that once either. All the time.'

The crowd held its breath. This was adding insult to injury with a vengeance.

'Why, you — you.'

Behind Reardon the Mexican girl disappeared hurriedly into the room labelled 'Office'. The doorway was no place for anyone if lead started to fly.

The stranger said, still quite quietly: 'I'm calling you, Reardon. Do we start even or do you usually like to have your guns out first?'

With a snort Reardon thrust his guns back into their holsters.

Matt Bronson said, thickly: 'Stay out of this, stranger. There's no cause for you to get killed on my account.'

The stranger smiled his frosty little smile; went on scratching the backs of his fingers.

'Who says I'm going to get killed?'

Even if nobody said it, it was what everyone was thinking. Most of them had seen Lew Reardon in action before. He was fast — devilishly fast. And accurate with it. A big bull of a man who could pump hot lead faster and straighter than any other man in that part of Texas. And that's saying something. For the average Texan uses the barrel of a six-shooter as a toothing-aid.

He stood now, poised, tensed, crouching a little, his fingers crooked so that only a half-inch of lamplight showed between the fingertips and the butts of his guns. In contrast, the stranger looked negligent, indifferent.

Reardon's harsh voice said: 'Jud, toss a quarter into the air.' He looked straight at the stranger, his eyes hot dark pools under craggy brows. 'When it hits the floor — '

He didn't finish. There was no need to finish. The stranger nodded in agreement.

'Anything you say,' he said quietly.

Jud's clipped, precise voice said: 'Ready?'

They eyed each other steadily a moment, nodded together, then Reardon said: 'Yes — ready.'

There was a breathless hush as the quarter spun in the air, winking in the yellow lamplight — a hush that seemed to go on and on interminably. The coin hit the earth-packed floor with a faint tinkling sound.

In a flash Reardon was going for his guns. His hands moved so fast that the eye could hardly follow them, sweeping up from his hips in a single swift movement that ended in the crash of gunfire.

2

The stranger hardly seemed to move at all. When the moment of action was over he stood there as casually, as negligently, as before. But a wisp of smoke curled up from the barrels of the six-guns in his hands — and Reardon was staggering back, nursing a hand that dripped blood.

There was a gasp of admiration from a crowd that knew real gunplay when they saw it . . . then a shout from Matt Bronson.

Even as he shouted Jud Reardon was squeezing the trigger of the tiny, pearl-handled derringer he had brought from under the flap of his black jacket.

The stranger wheeled, moving sideways in a single lightning movement that had something cat-like in its quality. The bullet nicked the tip of one ear, sending blood coursing down his cheek. In the same instant his own guns were blasting, filling the big, lamp-lit room with sound and fury. A surprised look came over Jud Reardon's face. One hand scrabbled at his chest as though trying to tear out the burning pain inside. Then he fell forward across the card table. It gave way under him with a protest of rending wood.

'Sorry about that,' the stranger said, quietly. 'I don't like killing, but he gave me no option.'

Lew Reardon, still nursing his damaged hand, looked across at him with savage eyes.

'I suppose not killing me was an act of grace on your part,' he said between gritted teeth.

The stranger paused in the act of holstering his guns.

'Sure was,' he said. 'I could have killed you if I'd wanted.'

He said it not boastfully, but as a plain man will make a plain statement of fact. And there were many in the crowd who believed what he said.

It was Big Bill McTigue who summed up what many of them were thinking.

'Jeeze,' he said in a voice that was clearly audible. 'But that kid's fast — like a cougar.'

* * *

And that was how the Cougar Kid got his name — a name that was to come to mean something in the rough, roaring beef-empire of Texas, across the Red River in Oklahoma, in the bawdy, lusty, cattle-shipment district around Dodge City in Kansas, in the silver mines of Colorado, across in New Mexico and the deserts of Arizona, even over the Rio Grande in Mexico.

Far and wide he ranged on that big black of his in the days when land and grass were free to those bold enough to take it and strong enough to hold it; when guns were worn promiscuously — and worn for use, not ornament. Like most men of his kind, he was a law unto himself. What his real name was or where he came from, no one ever knew. But somewhere, sometime, he had learned to handle those white-butted Colts of his with a speed that baffled the eye and defied description. There were those who said he must have been born with guns in his hands. Which is palpably nonsense. But I know what they meant. When the Cougar Kid went into action those white-butted guns seemed almost to leap up to meet his hands as though they were a part of his living tissue, recipients of the same messages that coursed from his brains to his fingers.

I knew him well. Or as well as anyone could ever hope to know the Cougar Kid, for no one could be quite sure what went on behind that blank, raw-boned face and those granite-chip eyes.

He was a hard man, a tough man, a killer if the occasion required — but always a fair man.

It was his sense of fair play which

won him respect even among those who hated him; those whose paths he crossed as he made and lost three separate fortunes: a fortune in cattle, a fortune in silver, a fortune in oil. But he lost all three, for he was always willing to pit everything he possessed — with the solitary exception of his guns and that beloved rangy black he rode — on the flick of a card or the roll of a dice.

The name he was given that night in the Golden Nugget saloon in Come Lucky stuck to him all his life. Somehow, it seemed to fit him like a glove. Not only on account of his speed with his guns. There was something of a cougar, too, about the way he looked and moved. The piercing intensity of those deepset eyes; the solid chunkiness of his shoulders; the panther-like slimness of his hips . . . with something of the big cat, too, in the way he was most tense, most poised, when apparently most relaxed.

That night, in the Nugget, he was at the outset of the strange, wild, adventurous career he was to carve out for himself on the cattle plains of the great southwest.

There are some who say that he tangled with Lew Reardon deliberately — to draw attention to himself — to let folk know that he had come to stay. I wouldn't know about that. But if he did have the intention of drawing attention to himself he succeeded better than he knew . . . and the wonder is that he ever lived on to make and lose those three separate fortunes.

*   *   *

Come Lucky, like many another western town-ships of the time, had come into existence for no better reason than that it was a convenient centre for the cattle ranchers of the area; a convenient gathering point for cattle to start the long, arduous eighty-day trek north to the rail centre at Dodge City for shipment east. It consisted of little more than one long, narrow, sunbaked street, flanked by wooden catwalks and hitching rails. There were perhaps half a hundred ramshackle woodbuilt houses, a smithy, a general store, an hotel of sorts, a barber shop, the Golden Nugget — and Jumbo Jordan's place. The lettering on the frosted glass window of Jordan's office gave it the impressive name of The Texas Range-Owners' Protection Association, but everyone in Come Lucky knew it simply as Jumbo Jordan's place.

The west, in those tough, hard, lawless days, bred a lot of honest-to-God, straight-shooting men. Men, who were tough, but honest along with their toughness. Men like the Cougar Kid. It also spawned a few like Jumbo Jordan, who were tough without being honest, out for easy money without being very particular how they went about getting it. Jumbo Jordan was tough, rotten, clever. Clever the way a rattlesnake is clever. He devised the good old protection racket long before the mobsters of Chicago ever heard of the word.

It was easy enough. The only law was the law of the six-gun. What you had was yours — for just as long as you could hold it. Which saw rancher pitted against rancher, with the big ranches hiring far more cowboys than they needed for their head of cattle — the additional hands being lawless hotheads whose only saving grace was their ability to handle a gun.

In all this Jumbo Jordan saw an opportunity for himself. The Texas Range-Owners' Protection Association was his idea. On its payroll was a small private army of the fastest gunmen of the south-west. If you were a rancher, you paid — and paid handsomely — to have the benefit of Jordan's protection. If you didn't pay, you very soon found out that you needed that protection. The subscription rates were high. Jordan's men protected the herds when they were driven north to the railhead — at a dollar for every steer in the drive. A drive that moved off without paying never got there. Poisoned water-holes, rustlers . . . Jordan would shrug his big shoulders when he heard the news, purse his thick lips, say: 'It only goes to show.'

It was the same on the actual ranges. If Jordan wasn't protecting you, your cattle vanished, your hands met up with lead poisoning, your fences were thrown down, maybe your ranchhouse burned down over your head . . . Small wonder that most ranchers — the little men in particular — chose to pay for protection rather than suddenly find themselves in need of it.

News of the affair in the Nugget reached the ears of Jumbo Jordan almost as soon as it had happened as did news of almost every other happening of note. Jordan had a good espionage network. He found it paid. Now he sat scratching his fat, stubbly chin and pondering how he might best use this new gunfighter who had drifted into Come Lucky. Jordan could always use a good gunfighter — and this man they were calling the Cougar Kid must be good to have shot it out with the Reardon brothers and come off best. Jordan, himself, would have thought twice about tangling with the Reardons.

Presently Jordan came ponderously to his feet, signed to Comanche Bill Tucson to follow him, and made his way along Come Lucky's solitary street to the saloon. Order had been more or less restored. The games of chance were in action again — save for the empty baize-topped card table in the corner. Jud Reardon's body was already on its way to Boot Hill, and Lew Reardon was in the back room having his damaged fin bandaged by the dark-eyed Lila.

The Cougar Kid leaned against the bar, one foot on the brass rail, sipping his third rye. If the big mirror at the back of the bar showed him any sign of the approach of Jumbo Jordan and Comanche Bill his pale, thin, expressionless face gave no sign of it.

The bar creaked as Jumbo leaned his twenty-stone against it.

'Have one on me,' he invited.

The Kid turned and looked at him through hard eyes.

'Why?' he asked uncompromisingly.

It was an answer which would have disconcerted most men. But not Jumbo Jordan. He signed to the bar-tender, caught the bottle that came skimming down, poured himself a drink, passed the bottle to Comanche Bill. 'Suit yourself,' he said to the Kid with a shrug of his massive shoulders.

The Kid smiled that frosty smile of his. 'I usually do.'

Jumbo downed his liquor; poured out some more.

'Hear you shot it out with Lew Reardon,' he said, presently. 'They call you the Cougar Kid, don't they?'

It was the first time the Kid had heard the name the inhabitants of Come Lucky had already bestowed on him.

'One name's as good as another,' he said.

Jumbo gave a deep-throated chuckle.

'Maybe you've got something there.'

He paused, sipping his liquor. Then he said: 'You just passing through or you figurin' on stopping around?'

'That's my business,' said the Kid.

The reply would have been offensive except for the quiet way he uttered it. Even so, it was offensive enough for Comanche Bill Tucson. Something round and small and hard bored into the centre of the Kid's back.

'When the boss asks a question, you answer,' he said, meaningly.

Jumbo Jordan could have sworn afterwards that the Kid didn't move as much as an eyelid. His right hand was in full view the whole time, his fingers curled round his glass of liquor. But something hard suddenly burrowed a clear two inches into the load of fat around Jordan's middle. It was Jordan's own gun, which had somehow skedaddled clean out of its own holster and found its way into the Kid's left hand.

The Kid said, quietly: 'Tell this hired gunpoke of yours to take that thing away from my back.' A prod of the gun-barrel which was burrowing itself into Jumbo's stomach made the rest of his meaning abundantly clear.

Jumbo said with excessive heartiness: 'Put that thing away, Comanche. The Kid don't have to answer unless he wants.'

Comanche Bill couldn't see the gun pointing at Jordan's middle. He looked puzzled. But he did as he was told. The men Jordan employed usually did as they were told. If they didn't, they were found one bright morning staring into the middle distance with eyes which didn't appreciate the view.

'That's better,' said the Kid, as the pressure of Comanche's gun vanished from his back. He smiled frostily and handed back Jumbo Jordan's gun. 'Yours, I think,' he said, cynically.

Jumbo thrust the heavy Colt back into its holster.

'I could use a man like you,' he said.

The Kid studied him closely over the rim of his glass.

'Doing what?'

'Gunfighting.'

'What sort of gunfighting?'

Jumbo waved a deprecating hand.

'Does it matter? You'd be well paid.'

The Kid said again: 'What sort of gunfighting?'

Jumbo's fat face wreathed in what was meant to be an honest, friendly, open smile.

'Look, friend,' he said, 'there's a lot of trouble in these hyar parts. This is new territory and the law is way behind the rest of us in getting here. The cattle-men need protection. I give it them.' He prodded the top of the bar with a big, stubby forefinger. 'I run the Texas Range-Owners' Protection Association. Most of the cattlemen subscribe and my men protect their interests. If there's any rus-tling, we root the rustlers out. When the herds go north for shipment, we go along with them. I'm sorta the marshal of this territory on a strictly commercial basis.'

All of which was true enough — as far as it went. The trouble was that it didn't go far enough. But the Cougar Kid wasn't to know that, of course.

'Where do I come in?' asked the Kid.

Jordan shrugged. 'I can always use a good gun-fighter,' he said. 'If you're sticking around, come and see me at my office in the morning.'

'Maybe I will,' said the Kid.

Jordan signed to Comanche Bill and the pair of them drifted out.

The Kid watched them go; shrugged and went on with his drinking. It seemed a reasonable enough proposition. He could do with the cash and it would give him a chance to look things over. There were fortunes to be made down here in the booming south-west for a man with guts and spirit — and capital. Working for Jordan would give him a chance to mark time while he looked round for ways of acquiring capital.

He didn't doubt that he would acquire it — somehow.

A man staggered across the saloon, cannoned against the outer doorpost, straightened himself up and went out through the swing-doors. It was Matt Bronson. Silly young fool! The Cougar Kid had little time for men who couldn't hold their liquor. He drank himself, heavily at times, but never so much that he lost control of his faculties. Any man in his right senses would have put his head under a pump and gone straight home after the gunplay earlier. But Bronson had gone on drinking; gone on gambling. Now, as he went out, he looked on the verge of collapse.

The Kid shrugged and told himself it was none of his business. All the same, he drank up and pushed through the swing-doors after Bronson. He seemed destined to go through life helping lame dogs over stiles. He smiled at the thought.

A full moon hung over the rangeland, turning the sage to silver and making Come Lucky's solitary street a ribbon of gold between the black wood-frame buildings. The Kid could see Bronson staggering along in the shadow of the buildings. He slipped and went sprawling.

The Kid caught up with him, slipped an arm about his shoulders and helped him to his feet.

'Where's your horse, feller?'

Bronson blinked at him owlishly.

'Ssssh' back — '

He pointed vaguely with a drunken forefinger. At that moment a buckboard came clattering the length of the street. A girl was driving it, her hair streaming in the wind, her hat blown back and caught by the cord around her throat. The moon turned her hair the colour of pure cornsilk. Bronson waved frantically, staggering unsteadily on his feet. Only the Kid's arm around his shoulders prevented him from falling again.

'Hiya, Gail — here I am — 'sme — '

The girl dragged the buckboard to a halt and jumped down from the driving seat.

'Oh, Matt,' she said, 'you've been drinking again.'

She was tall and slim, wearing breeches and a pink silk shirt open at the neck to reveal a white, soft throat. She caught her red bottom lip between firm white teeth.

Bronson staggered towards her, the Kid still supporting him.

'Just a drop or two, Gail, old dear. Nothing to make a song and dance about.'

The girl turned on the Kid.

'And you've been encouraging him, I suppose. Why hasn't he got the sense to stay away from you and your kind? You're no good to him.'

The Kid said, quietly: 'Just a moment, Mrs Bronson — '

'Miss Bronson,' the girl retorted, fiercely. 'Get on the buckboard, Matt, and I'll drive you home.'

Bronson shook his head, drunkenly.

'I can ride,' he said. 'I can ride.' He looked round. 'Where's my horse? Someone fetch that blasted horse.'

The girl said: 'You're in no condition to ride, Matt. Please climb into the buckboard.'

Bronson shook his head again with drunken obstinacy.

'Ain't gonna go no place — '

The Kid shouldered him towards the buckboard.

'Do as the lady says, feller.'

Bronson looked at him, grinning foolishly.

'The lady?' he said, thickly. 'What lady? That's no lady, sir — thass my sister.'

He went off into peals of drunken laughter.

There was only one way to settle things. The Kid let go of Bronson, stepped back a pace. Then, as Bronson swayed forwards, the Kid's fist flashed up straight to the point of the jaw. He caught Bronson as he fell, hoisted him over his shoulder and tossed him aboard the buckboard. He turned back to the girl.

'There he is, lady — all tucked up and ready for bed. Off you go now.'

The girl looked at him a moment.

'You brute,' she said. 'You great

brute. Hitting a drunken man like that.'

'Say, wait a minute, lady. Seems to me you're too all-fired steamed up — '

His hand caught at the sleeve of the silk shirt as she swung herself back into the driving seat.

'Leave go of me, you dirty no-good.'

She snatched her arm away from him, caught at the whip and before the Kid could do anything about it had lashed him full across the face.

'You stay away from my brother in the future,' she said, fiercely. 'You understand — you and all your kind.'

She lashed the horses harnessed to the buckboard as fiercely as she had lashed the Kid himself. They broke into a canter and the buckboard clattered away down the street. The Kid stood looking after it, caressing his slashed cheek. The young arm which wielded the whip had been a strong one. He shook his head. Women were just like cattle — you never could tell about either one of them.

3

The next day the Cougar Kid signed up to work for Jumbo Jordan. The set-up, once he got to know it, struck him as a little peculiar. But no more than that. Jordan had twenty-odd gunslingers working for him — as tough and wicked a bunch as you could find anywhere in the south-west. That didn't worry the Kid unduly. If you signed on a man for his ability to handle a gun, you had to take what else went along with it. What did puzzle him though was that the whole crew seemed to spend nearly all their time either drinking in the saloon or playing cards in the big ante-room adjoining Jumbo Jordan's office. He would have expected range guards to be doing just that — guarding the range. Patrolling the outlying grassland, keeping an eye on the waterholes, checking the hills for stray cattle that might fall an easy prey to rustlers. That they didn't struck him as a little peculiar, but it never occurred to him that there was anything downright dishonest about the set-up. The few honest folk of Come Lucky who could have told him what he had let himself in for didn't do so because they figured he already knew. The gunslingers who rode for Jumbo Jordan kept their mouths shut because Jumbo had told them to do just that.

Gail Bronson nearly let the cat out of the bag when he met her in Come Lucky two days after the gunplay in the Last Chance. The Kid had been buying shells for his white-butted sixguns in the town store. He was coming out as her dilapidated buckboard rattled to a halt outside. She jumped out, twined the reins round the hitching rail and ran up the wooden steps. She flushed when she saw the Kid.

'Why — er — Mister — '

The Kid didn't say anything. He could guess what was coming and saw no reason why he should help her out.

Her fingers played with the buttons of her silk shirt. She looked down.

'I guess I owe you some sort of an apology,' she said.

Still the Kid didn't say anything.

'My brother told me all about what happened that night after he sobered up. About how you shot it out with the Reardons on account of him. I guess I was pretty steamed up that night. Matt's kinda wild and I got worried, and when I saw the pair of you — '

She broke off.

The Kid said, coldly: 'Don't let it worry you any, Miss Bronson. I guess a pretty girl like you is entitled to take a slash at a common cowpoke once in awhile.'

Her colour deepened.

'I'm — I'm sorry,' she said.

Looking at him, she knew he was no common cowhand. The twin gunbelts around his waist told her that. But there was something else, too. Something about the way he held himself, an air of aloofness . . . a curious sort of something you might call breeding. He was not exactly good-looking, yet there was something about him that was incredibly fascinating. A curious mixture of boyishness and hard-won experience. She surprised herself thinking that she could very easily fall in love with a man like that. Her colour deepened still further.

Seeing it deepen, misjudging the reason, the Kid relented. He didn't pretend to understand women like Gail Bronson. Women like the Mexican, Lila, were more his line of country. You could love 'em and leave 'em — and that way you knew exactly where you were. But the Gail Bronson type wanted to see a man thrown and hogtied for life before they would consent to hand out as much as a kiss. No, he didn't understand them, but he could nevertheless appreciate them when they were as good-looking and clean-cut as Matt Bronson's sister.

His voice was no longer cold and edgy when he said: 'I'm sorry, too. For speaking to you thataway. I guess I understand just how you feel about that brother of yours.'

Her fingers twined themselves together. She said, almost as though speaking to herself: 'Matt's not bad — not really. Just weak. Easily led. Since Father died, having a ranch of his own — even if we do run only three hundred head of stock — has rather gone to his head.' She looked up. 'I'm very grateful for what you did for him the other night. Perhaps you'd care to ride out and see us at the Crazy Y sometime.'

She said it a little breathlessly and told herself that the uneasy thumping of her heart was simply due to driving the buckboard into town. But she didn't believe what she told herself.

The Kid said: 'That's mighty nice of you, Miss Bronson. I guess I'd like that.'

Gail said, hurriedly: 'Come any time you like. I — that is, Matt — would be pleased to see you. And if there's anything else we can do in return for what you did . . . '

The Kid shook his head.

'No — nothing, Miss Bronson. You don't need to think you owe me anything. I'd have done the same for anyone else.'

The girl looked at him. Yes, she thought — of course he would. He was that kind. A two-gun man, but honest, decent, thoughtful with it. Steady on, Gail Bronson, she told herself; you're getting a sight too emotional over a man you know nothing about. But it didn't stop her saying:

'If you want a job, there's always one for you at the Crazy Y.'

Afterwards she didn't know quite why she had said it. With only three hundred head of cattle, they didn't need more than one cowhand and Charlie Bennion already filled the bill. And yet she did know. She wanted this loose-limbed, haggard, hard-eyed stranger around the place.

'It's very kind of you, Miss Bronson, but I've already got a job — with Jumbo Jordan.'

The girl felt her heart give a sickening little lurch inside her. It just showed how wrong you could be. He was that kind — one of Jumbo Jordan's hired gunslingers. She hated Jumbo Jordan and all that he stood for with a peculiarly personal hatred — the hatred of a girl who can sense when a man lusts after her.

A shadow crossed her face.

'I see,' she said. That was all. But the Kid was susceptible to slight shades of meaning.

'What's wrong?' he asked. 'Why shouldn't I work for Jumbo Jordan?'

She didn't answer him. Instead she brushed past him.

'I've got to hurry back,' she said. 'Matt will be waiting for me.' And she slipped into the store. The Kid watched her go with narrowed eyes.

That meeting with Gail Bronson was the Kid's first real clue to the fact that the Jumbo Jordan set-up was perhaps not all that it pretended to be. He resolved to watch points carefully over the next few days, but it didn't get him anywhere. On the surface, at least, the Texas Range-Owners' Protection Association seemed all that it claimed to be.

But if the Kid was not aware of what was going on below the surface, plenty of others were. Particularly the ranchers, who, with the next big cattle drive up the Chisholm Trail to Dodge City only a few weeks off, found themselves receiving a call from Jumbo Jordan. A dollar a head was Jumbo's price for protecting the herd on the drive north. Not that he proposed to hand out any real protection. But backbones were stiffening against him. It had been a bad year for the cattlemen and for many of the smaller ones, like Matt Bronson, that dollar a head could make all the difference between a profit and a loss on the year's working. There were several who called Jumbo's bluff.

He sat over a bottle of whisky with Comanche Bill, thumbing his thick bottom lip as he considered the problem. On the table in front of him was a scrawled list of the ranches in the area. Some were ticked off. Those with ticks against them were the ones who had stumped up. They were in the majority. But there were enough unticked ones to make things difficult if word got around. Someone had got to be taught a sharp lesson — as an example to others. Then perhaps the others would come to heel.

He said as much to Comanche Bill.

Comanche's face split into what he fancied to be a grin. What lay ahead promised to be work after his own heart. He took one of his Colts from its scabbard and squinted suggestively along the barrel.

'Who's it gonna be?' he asked.

Jumbo drummed on the table with his thick fingers.

'The Crazy Y,' he said presently.

'Chicken-feed stuff,' sneered Comanche. 'They only run three hundred head; only one hand.' Jumbo nodded.

'That's just what I've got in mind,' he said. 'One man is soon dealt with. And however small they are, they'll serve as

45

an example to others.'

He had another reason, too — Gail Bronson. But he didn't tell Comanche Bill Tucson that. Jordan wanted Gail Bronson, wanted her as he had never wanted any other woman. Something about her gripped him whenever he saw her, seemed to edge up on him and crawl right under his skin. Firing the Crazy Y would be a means of killing two birds with one stone.

But Comanche was no fool. He sensed a great deal more than Jumbo had any reason to suppose.

He tilted his chair back at an angle. 'What about the girl?' he asked.

There was a moment's silence. Then Jumbo said: 'What about her?'

Comanche rolled himself a cigarette; ran the paper along the tip of his tongue.

'We can't afford to have any witnesses,' he said.

Jumbo grinned — an unpleasant grin.

'There won't be any. When the job's

over we'll take the girl into the Sierras.'

Comanche gazed at him through narrowed lids.

'I don't like it,' he said. 'I don't like it one — '

Jumbo's big fat hand came down hard on the table. Jumbo, himself, came to his feet — a great mountain of a man, twenty stone of bone and muscle and solid fat. In contrast, Comanche Bill, his dark face and high cheekbones betraying Indian blood somewhere back along the line, looked weedy and insignificant.

'Get this and get it straight,' said Jumbo. 'What you like and what you don't like don't rate with me. I'm the boss of this outfit and what I says — goes.'

Comanche shrugged.

'Sure. Sure. I ain't aiming to tangle with you, Jumbo.'

However the look in his dark eyes didn't go all the way beneath his words. He drew on his cigarette; let the smoke trickle out of his nostrils.

'Who does the job?' he asked.

'Just you and me,' said Jumbo. 'And the Cougar Kid.'

Comanche raised his eyebrows in a quizzical gesture.

'Think he'll toe the line?'

Jumbo's fat face wreathed in a grin.

'He'll toe the line all right — afterwards. We'll leave him with the horses. He won't know what's afoot till it's all over. By that time he'll have no option but to string along.'

Comanche grinned back.

'You got brains, Jumbo,' he said. 'I'll say that for you. It takes brains to think up a thing like that. When do we do the job?'

Jumbo pulled his gunbelt in a couple of notches.

'Now,' he said. 'Tonight.'

48

4

Moonlight turned the sage into a sea of silver as the Cougar Kid cantered his big black along the trail behind the ponderous bulk of Jumbo Jordan and the slim, slight figure of Comanche Bill Tucson. In the distance, where the sage ended, the Sierras rose in purple grandeur, lifting crest upon crest high into the heavens to meet the dark cloak of night. The Kid felt curiously contented. Maybe the softness of the night did that. Maybe the knowledge that something was in the offing. He was impatient, always, when life rolled by easily and monotonously, but a curious contentment crept over him whenever action was imminent.

Ahead of him, Jumbo held up his hand and the Kid reined his big black to a standstill. The buildings of a ranch stood out in silhouette against the

49

moonlight It was the Crazy Y — but the Cougar Kid didn't know that.

Jumbo said: 'You stay here with the horses. Comanche and I've got a call to make.'

He and Comanche slid from their saddles and tossed the Kid their hitching reins. The darkness in the shadow of the ranch buildings swallowed them up as they walked away with that curious rolling gait the cowboy finds himself forced to adopt when he uses his own two legs.

Jumbo said, once they were out of hearing: 'You take the bunkhouse, Comanche. There's only the one guy to deal with. No gunplay, mind. I don't want the Cougar Kid to know a thing until he's in this as deep as we are.'

Comanche nodded. His hand went to his rump and something cold and bright gleamed for an instant in the moonlight. He slid away silently into the darkness.

Jumbo clumped up the steps to the main door of the ranch. His right hand wore a Colt. His left took down the latch. He kicked open the door with his foot and went inside.

The main room of the ranch was long and low with a plank floor; sparsely furnished. An oil lamp burned on the table. Gail Bronson sat at the table, reading. She was no longer in riding kit and it was surprising how much more feminine she looked. She wore a dress of yellow gingham and her cornsilk hair was done up with a ribbon of the same colour.

She looked up and saw Jordan; saw the Colt in his big fist. Her heart gave a nervous little jump, but she was determined not to let Jumbo see she was scared.

She said, coldly: 'Do you usually walk into other people's places without knocking?'

She wanted to go on and say more, to talk and keep talking, babble nonsense, anything to fight down that sick feeling that filled the pit of her stomach like a hard lump. She knew why Jordan was there. She had been present on his previous call when her brother had told him to get to hell; that there would be no more subscriptions to the Range-Owners' Protection Association from the Crazy Y.

Jordan ignored her remark. He closed the door behind him and stood where he would be in a position to cover anyone who might come bustin' in.

'Where's your brother?' he said.

Gail knew where Matt was all right — over at the Double Diamond. Pete Farman, boss of the Double Diamond, had called a meeting of all the small ranchers who couldn't — or wouldn't — subscribe any more to keep Jumbo Jordan in luxury. But she wasn't going to tell Jordan that. She looked at the clock on the wooden mantelshelf. Matt wouldn't be back till morning. She could expect no help from that quarter.

'I said where's your brother?'

Gail knew she had to lie.

She pushed her chair back and came to her feet.

'How should I know? Down at the Nugget, I suppose. That's where he usually goes, gambling and drinking his money away like any no-good cow-hand.'

Jumbo Jordan shook his big head.

'You know he ain't been there since the night Reardon got killed.' He took a step towards her. 'Think again — or do I have to do something to make you think.' He moistened his thick lips in anticipation.

'Keep away from me, you big slob.'

'Spirit, eh? I like a girl with spirit.'

He moved towards her. Gail whirled and raced across the room. A Winchester was propped up in the far corner. Jordan guessed her intention and moved to intercept her. He moved surprisingly quickly for a man of his bulk. His big arm swept out, caught her round the waist, lifted her, struggling, clear of the floor.

Gail hammered at his face with her fists.

'Let me go. Let me go.'

Jordan only grinned and pressed his thick lips hard on hers. The girl felt a shudder run through. He was vile . . . vile.

The door clattered open. Jordan let go of her and turned.

It was Comanche Bill Tucson.

He said: 'There ain't no one in the bunkhouse, Jumbo.'

'Try the rest of the buildings,' Jumbo snarled.

'I have. The whole lot. There ain't no one about at all.'

Gail Bronson lay back against the wall where Jordan had thrown her. She was half-dazed and her face white. She knew where their solitary cowhand — Charlie Bennion — was. Down by Medicine Creek. With any luck he ought to be back around now. If only she could stall them, somehow.

Jordan looked at Comanche Bill; nodded. 'OK,' he said. 'Get on with it.'

Gail Bronson pushed herself clear of the wall. Her head was swimming, but she forced words to her lips.

'What are you going to do?'

She didn't need to ask.

Comanche Bill moved towards the fire, plucked out one of the burning brands, carried it across towards the windows.

Gail rushed at Jumbo and tore at his sleeve.

'You can't do that to us,' she said. 'You can't. This ranch is all we've got. We'll pay.'

Jumbo shook his head.

'You should have thought of that the other day,' he said.

Gail let go of his arm and raced towards the writing desk. She threw down the top, rooted in the pigeon-holes.

'Here,' she said. 'Take the money. Only leave us the ranch.'

The small leather bag jingled as she threw it on the floor at his feet.

Jumbo said: 'It's too late. I don't want your money.'

She leaned back against the desk. 'What do you want then?'

'You.'

The look in his hot, dark eyes made his meaning plain. The tip of Gail's tongue showed between her lips, strikingly red against the whiteness of her face. Her skin seemed completely drained of colour.

'No,' she said. 'No. You can't mean it.'

Jumbo grinned.

'That's the way it's going to be, sweetheart, whether you like it or not.'

He nodded at Comanche Bill. The half-caste gunslinger applied the burning brand to the curtains. A tongue of flame licked up the material. Gail saw it happen with hopeless eyes. Then she saw that Jumbo Jordan was coming towards her.

'No,' she cried. 'No.'

His hand reached out for her.

'Nooooo.' The word died away into a high-pitched scream.

Comanche Bill moved towards the door.

'Let's get out a here,' he said. 'This

place'll burn like a tinder-box.'

Outside, astride his big black, the Cougar Kid watched that red flicker of flame run up the curtains with puzzled eyes. For a second he failed to appreciate what was happening. Then, as Gail Bronson's scream rent the night air, he slipped from the saddle and ran towards the ranch-house, his white-butted Colts hefted high as he took the steps leading up to the main door in a single bound.

Someone else heard the scream, too — Charlie Bennion, the Crazy Y's solitary hired hand, cantering home across the range three hundred yards off. His face, too, wore a puzzled expression for a few seconds after he heard it. Then he was digging in his spurs, standing in the stirrups, urging his horse to its fullest extent.

He came round the corner of the ranch buildings just as the Cougar Kid went bounding up the steps; just as the door opened and Comanche Bill and Jumbo Jordan came running out. Gail

Bronson was mercifully unconcious as Jordan held her in his big arms.

'What the hell goes on?' demanded the Cougar Kid.

'There's been an accident,' said Jumbo. 'The place is ablaze.'

He might have got away with the bluff but for Comanche Bill — and Charlie Bennion. As Bennion's horse skidded to a standstill and the cow-puncher threw himself from the saddle, Comanche fired.

The Cougar Kid knew then that what had happened was no accident. All his uncertain doubts and suspicions of the Jumbo Jordan outfit returned, hardened, crystallised.

Charlie Bennion staggered as Comanche's shot took him in the shoulder; fired back; threw himself flat in the shadow of the ranch-house and went on firing. Guns blazed in the darkness as the first tongue of flame splintered the ranch-house window and leaped out into the night.

The Cougar Kid's first volley got

Comanche Bill, hitting him in the stomach, slamming him back against the hitching rail. The Kid whirled to cope with Jumbo Jordan.

The big man was backing away, the girl held in front of him. His gun barked under her arm. The Kid felt the heat of the shell as it cut the air nearby.

He held his fire. The girl was between him and his target.

Jumbo kept on backing up. The ranch was well ablaze by now, the flames throwing a ruddy glare far across the rangeland. Of dry, sunbaked timber, the place burned as Comanche Bill had said it would — like a tinder-box. A roaring sound heralded the collapse of part of the roof.

Silhouetted against the glare, the Cougar Kid made a perfect target. But Jumbo Jordan was in no position to take advantage of the fact. The girl's body hampered him as much as it shielded him and his shots went wild.

But Charlie Bennion was still firing and thinking. To him the Cougar Kid was part and parcel of the crowd who were carrying off Miss Gail.

One arm hung limp and he was losing blood rapidly, but his other hand could still handle a Colt. He hefted it; fired. The shell creased across the Kid's head, hitting him with all the force of a kicking mule, and leaving a faint line of blood. A black pit opened up ahead of him. He dived in.

As the Kid fell flat on his face, Jumbo Jordan turned and ran. Charlie Bennion staggered to his feet and tried to run after him. Twice he collapsed. Jordan tossed the unconscious girl across the front of his horse and climbed into the saddle. Bennion heard the thud of hoofs as the animal was spurred into a gallop.

Turning, Bennion staggered back towards his own horse. But terrified by the flames of the burning ranch-house, the frightened animal had plunged off into the night. There was another crash as the rest of the roof caved in. A shower of sparks settled, and around the ranch-house patches of dried grass began to burn. Reeling unsteadily, Bennion made his way round the burning ranch-house to the corral. Weak from loss of blood, it took him ten minutes to catch one of the terrified animals and saddle it. Slumped in the saddle, Charlie pulled the head of his horse round and trotted it across the range towards the Double Diamond.

5

Nearly three dozen men were crowded into the big main room of the Double Diamond ranch-house. They had been there for three hours, arguing, haggling, but it hadn't really gotten them any place. There were too many weak spirits among them; too many who were afraid to buck the Jumbo Jordan outfit.

One of them, Zeke Martin, a tall, thin-faced man with a slight stoop, expressed the views of several when he said: 'It's all right talking, but talk don't get us any place. Jordan's got us hogtied and he knows it. We ain't no match for those gunslingers of his. I don't like paying any more'n you do, but I know when I'm well off.'

Pete Farman thudded the tabletop with his clenched fist.

'Well, I ain't paid and I ain't paying,' he said. 'I've paid long enough. I'd be a rich man now but for the money I've forked out to Jumbo Jordan.'

'Me, too!' echoed half a dozen voices, but they were in the minority.

Matt Bronson said: 'I've not paid either, but only because I couldn't. Now I've got to fight Jordan whether I like it or not.'

Someone said: 'How do we know it is Jordan for certain?'

There was a bellow of laughter at that.

Pete Farman said: 'Of course it's Jordan. Maybe we can't prove it — and there ain't no law around these parts if we could — but everyone in his right senses knows it's Jordan. If you don't pay, something happens. Well, I'm fed up with paying and I'm gonna fight.'

'It won't get you any place, Pete,' said Zeke Martin.

'Maybe not, but it'll get me my self-respect back, and that's something worth having. I've been without it too long.'

Another thin chorus of agreement.

'What do you say, then?' demanded Matt. 'Are you with me or not?'

There was a chorus of 'Aye', but there were also many who shook their heads.

Pete Farman thudded the tabletop again. 'I tell you — '

He broke off as someone hammered with a gun-butt against the outer door. Eyes narrowed; several hands reached for guns.

'Jumbo Jordan,' someone murmured.

Farman silenced him with a glare.

'Don't be a lily-livered fool. How would Jumbo know we were meeting here?'

But his own hand was clenched tightly about his gunbutt as he moved towards the door.

He jerked it open. Charlie Bennion staggered in. His gun fell from his grasp and he went sprawling.

'Get some water,' rapped Farman.

They threw it over him; forced some whiskey past his clenched teeth. When Charlie Bennion swam back to consciousness Matt Bronson was bending over him.

'What is it, Charlie?'

Charlie gestured vaguely with his left arm.

'The Crazy Y — burnt out.' There was a gasp of apprehension.

'See where bucking Jumbo Jordan gets you,' said Zeke Martin.

Matt Bronson had the wounded cowboy by the shoulders; was shaking him, unaware of what he did.

'Gail?' he said. 'Where's Gail? What happened to her?'

'They got her.'

'She's dead. My God! You mean she's dead.'

Bennion shook his head; said dazedly:

'Not dead. They got her. Took her. I got two of them.'

'Who was it? Answer me, Charlie. Who was it? Jumbo Jordan?'

Charlie spoke thickly.

'I think so. Looked like him. Can't be sure.'

Pete Farman leaped on to a chair.

'D'you hear that, boys? Jumbo Jordan's kidnapped Gail Bronson. Now are you going to fight?'

There wasn't a man in the room who didn't know and like Gail Bronson. Many of the older ones had known her when she had first come out west, a pigtailed youngster knee-high to a grasshopper. They admired her for her pluck in staying on to help her brother run the ranch after their father died. They knew how she had fought against her brother's love of drinking and gambling: And not a few of the younger ones thought they were in love with her. The knowledge that she was in danger caused a change of heart on the part of many.

The chorus of 'Aye' was louder, more full-throated.

There were still a few abstainers — Zeke Martin and his kind — but they didn't matter any more.

Peter Farman jumped down from his chair. 'Well, what the hell are we waiting for? Let's get saddled up.' There was a general stampede in the direction of the door. The abstainers were left to look after the injured cowboy, and three minutes later, with Matt Bronson and Farman in the lead, the bunch of horsemen spurred their mounts across the range in the direction of the Crazy Y.

The ranch-house was a burnt-out shell by the time they got there. Part of the outer walls remained standing, but the rest was just so much charred, blackened wood which still smouldered red in parts as the wind fanned it and gave off little wisps of smoke, Comanche Bill's body lay where it had fallen — unrecognisable now. When the veranda collapsed a burning post had fallen full across the body, cremating it.

The Cougar Kid had been more fortunate. The heat had singed his eyebrows and hair, but no more than that. The big rawboned black he rode had found him and dragged him out of harm's way. Most cow-ponies wouldn't have gone within a hundred yards of the blaze. But the black was different — gifted with almost the intelligence of a human being. Which was why the Kid prized it so highly despite the fact that it looked like a lumbering carthorse in contrast to the normal cow-pony. It hadn't the burst of speed of a cow-pony either, but it had a staying power that was unequalled in the south-west.

It stood over the Kid now, head down, using its big tongue to lick him back into consciousness. The Kid stirred uneasily; tried to sit up.

'Hey,' yelled Pete Farman. 'This one ain't dead.'

Matt Bronson came running from the smouldering ruins of the ranch-house. The others gathered round, hands on guns, ugly looks on their faces.

Farman dropped on one knee, seized the Kid by his scorched shirt, jerked him into a sitting position. The Kid's head fell wearily forward. Farman jerked it upright again, slapped him crisply across the face.

'Listen, you. Where's Jumbo Jordan?'

The Cougar Kid shook his head. His

lips were blackened and cracked; his tongue felt like a great furry caterpillar. Presently he managed to get the words out.

'Don't know.'

Farman shook him again, angrily, brutally.

'Don't give us that,' he snarled. 'You were here. Where's Jumbo taken the girl — Miss Bronson?'

The Kid shook his head again.

'I tell you I don't know.'

Someone in the crowd said: 'He knows all right. He's one of Jordan's men. I've seen the two of them around together.'

They crowded forward, murmuring. Honest, normally good-natured, they were in an ugly mood. They had stood about all they were prepared to stand from Jumbo Jordan and his so-called Range-Owners' Protection Association. The firing of the Crazy Y and the kidnapping of Gail Bronson had been the last straw.

Looking round them, the Kid saw

only one face not suffused with hatred and contempt — Matt Bronson's. Bronson's face betrayed mixed emotions. In his eyes anger warred with the knowledge that this was a man who had saved his life that night in the Golden Nugget. For the rest, the Kid could see no hope of mercy in the hard, cold eyes that regarded him steadily as dawn sent its probing fingers over the distant foothills.

'Look,' he said, angrily. 'I've told you I don't know and there's an end of it. I didn't know what Jordan had in mind when we came out here — '

Angry murmurings cut short what he was saying.

'A likely tale.'

'Who the hell does he think we are — a pack of greenhorns?'

'String the skunk up.'

The idea caught on, materialised, grew. Angry hands seized the Kid. His eyes were suddenly cold and frosty, no longer quite human. He jerked his arm free. One set of fingers scratched the back of the others.

'I've told you the truth. If you want to argue it out . . . let's go.'

His hands flashed towards the gun-holsters at his hips. In the same instant he threw himself forwards and upwards on to his feet. And only then did he realize that it was all a waste of time. Someone had thought of that. His prized white-butted Colts were no longer in their holsters.

'String the coyote up.'

The Kid lashed out as they closed in on him. He had the satisfaction of feeling the thud as his fist jarred on bone, of seeing tight-drawn skin split open like an over-ripe melon. Then they were swarming over him, hitting him, kicking him, forcing him down. His head swam under a rain of blows. A fist like a sledge-hammer thudded into his ribs. A gun-butt crashed down on the back of his head. He fell forward on to his knees.

His arms were caught and jerked to the back of him. Cord bit into his wrists.

Someone said: 'Where's that horse of his?'

Dizzy, sick, his head swimming, the Kid felt himself lifted on to the back of his big black as though it was something happening in a dream. He felt his feet being roped together under the black's belly. Then something settled about his neck.

He shook his head, fighting off the dizziness which threatened to swamp him.

Wrists and feet lashed, a rope about his neck, he knew only too well what the next move was. This was Judge Lynch's law coming into its own. The Kid had seen it happen a score of times — to others. Most had deserved it. A few hadn't. But there was nothing anyone could do about those that hadn't deserved it. Once justice gets out of hand there is no stopping it. Now it was happening to him. The next move was a tall cottonwood tree, with the rope thrown over one branch and the end tied to another. A slash of the ropes that bound his legs, a smack at the rump of the big black, and another body would dangle until the buzzards picked it clean.

The Kid was under no illusions about things. It wasn't a particularly pleasant way to die — particularly if the jerk of the rope failed to break a man's neck. Then, at best, he could only hope for slow strangulation. At worst, for the sharp beaks of the buzzards tearing living tissue from the bones around which it was moulded.

Without his guns, there was no way out — unless he could talk his way out. And the faces that surrounded him, as the big black was urged into a jog-trot, didn't look particularly amenable to persuasion.

The sun came up over the Sierras in a great round ball of fire. The Kid could feel the heat of it on the back of his neck. He wondered if he would ever feel it again.

There was laughter a-plenty from those who rode with the Kid that sunrise; rough jokes. But the jokes sounded forced and the laughter rang hollow. It is one thing to kill a man in hot blood, to shoot him in fair gunplay, and quite another to go through with a lynching cold-bloodedly and dispassionately. The jokes and the laughter were an echo of nerves rubbed raw by the strain of the occasion.

They came to a stream; forded it. On the far side, a little way down, was a grove of willows. They rode into it, silent now, the jokes over, the moment for action arrived. The moment which was to see a man launched into Eternity.

With sombre, listless eyes, the Kid watched the end of the rope tossed over the limb of a cottonwood tree that stood in the grove; felt the loop tighten about his neck as the big black stirred under him.

'Steady, boy,' he said in a whisper.

The black stood motionless as a statue.

There was a slash with a knife and he

felt his legs come free. The ranchers stood and looked at one another, each waiting for the next to deliver that fatal slap to the rump of the rawboned black.

One said, in a high-pitched voice which betrayed the way he was feeling: 'OK. Let's get it over with.'

He took a step forward as he spoke; raised his hand.

6

'No!'

The exclamation was jerked from the throat of Matt Bronson. He sat his horse a short distance off, watching all that happened with worried eyes. Now he rode forward, shaking his head.

Pete Farman said: 'What the hell's got into you, Matt? It was your sister, your ranch-house.'

'I know — ' Bronson broke off; licked his lips. He looked round at the hard-set faces which regarded hirn. He knew it was no good trying to explain to them how he felt; pointing out that the Kid had saved his life. Their blood was up — and someone had got to pay. They might not like what they were doing, but they were determined to go through with it.

He said: 'Stringing him up won't get my sister back.'

Farman said: 'We know that, but — '

Matt Bronson cut in on him.

'Look,' he said. 'The only way to find out what's happened to my sister is to persuade this guy to talk.'

'He ain't shown much sign of being cooperative so far.'

'Maybe not. But once he's strung up there's no chance at all. Let's take him into town with us and see if we can't get something out of him.'

'Why go into town, anyway?'

'Because Jumbo Jordan's office is there. Maybe Jumbo himself. Maybe he's gonna try to bluff things out as he has so often in the past.'

Farman said, angrily: 'Well, this sure is one time he ain't gonna get away with it.'

There was an angry murmur of assent.

Bronson said: 'Either way, it does no harm to keep this guy alive until we see what's what. Maybe Jumbo's there. If he's not, I think I can persuade the Kid to tell us where he is.'

The silence which greeted him showed that the pendulum was beginning to swing the other way. Tempers were dying down; reason beginning to take over.

Pete Farman said: 'What makes you think you can get him to talk, Matt?'

Matt Bronson shrugged his slim shoulders. 'I dunno, Pete. I just think I can.'

The Kid heard it all with his face strictly dead-pan. It might not have concerned him for all the feeling he permitted to show in those granite-chip eyes. His life still hung in the balance, and it would have been the easiest thing in the world for him to have said something to help tilt the balance the right way. 'Look, fellers, I know I rode for Jumbo Jordan, but I didn't know the truth about things — honest to God, I didn't. I thought Jumbo was what he claimed to be. I didn't know he planned to fire the Crazy Y and kidnap Miss Bronson. I thought it was just a business call.'

That was the sort of thing he could have said easily enough. And now that tempers were beginning to fade it might have made sense. But the Kid didn't say that. To him, the idea savoured too much of begging for his life, of pleading for mercy. He was proud, the Cougar Kid — too damned proud by half; arrogant with it. More than once, as now, that stubborn, inborn pride of his nearly cost him his life. He was a big man — in spirit, if not in stature — and that damned pride of his was the one weakness that kept him from being a really great man during those wild, lawless years when the south-west was his stamping-ground.

So it was left to Matt Bronson to carry the burden of pleading the Kid's cause. Some among that small, hard-bitten crowd were convinced by what he said. But others — noticeably the ones who had originally hung back from fighting Jumbo Jordan — were out for an easy victory. The Cougar Kid was one of Jordan's men. OK, then — string him up. It was as easy as that.

One of them voiced that opinion.

'He won't talk. Not in a million years. I know the breed.'

Bronson said, firmly: 'I still want to try.'

'To hell with what you want, Matt. String the buzzard up and have done with it.'

There was a surge forward — and those who surged forward found themselves looking into the single eye of Matt Bronson's four-five.

Afterwards Matt Bronson, himself, wasn't quite sure what made him do it. Some mistaken sense of honour, perhaps. The Kid had saved his life. So he must save the Kid's. And underneath it all was the feeling that he could persuade the Kid to talk if he could get him alone some place. His bottom lip trembled a little. He felt he could do with a shot of liquor to steady his nerve. But the hand that held the four-five didn't tremble.

'I say no. She was my sister and I've

got a right to have my say. The Kid's going into Come Lucky with us. Any guy that thinks otherwise can settle it with me.'

That held them.

Pete Farman caressed a stubbly chin.

'Sure, Matt, if that's the way you feel about it — OK.' He turned in the saddle. 'Cut him down, boys.'

Someone cut the rope which ran over the limb of the cottonwood, took the loop from about the Kid's neck and lashed his feet under the belly of the black again. With someone holding the hitching-rein of the black, he rode with the whole bunch into Come Lucky.

The moment the procession hit the one and only street of that ugly little town the townsfolk knew that something was in the wind.

The hard, set faces of Pete Farman and the others told them that. So did the fact that in the centre of the crowd, securely roped, rode the Cougar Kid. Everyone knew that the Kid worked for Jumbo Jordan and news of what was afoot ran ahead of them with the speed of a prairie fire.

Folk crowded to doorways, and then, as realisation dawned, disappeared as quickly as they had come. Doors were slammed and bolts thrust home. A woman, skirts billowing, ran across the dusty street ahead of them to grab up a kid playing on the sidewalk and vanish with the youngster into the nearest convenient doorway. Ed Parsons, who ran the dry goods store, hurried out, to thrust the shutters in place over his plateglass windows.

There was no sheriff nearer than Abilene. If, indeed, there was one there. In the south-west, in those days, a sheriff was apt to be here today and gone tomorrow. A feller who stayed just so long as he could wield the law better than anyone he happened to cross.

Jumbo Jordan's office was at the far end of the street, beyond the Golden Nugget, and long before the procession reached there the street was a silent, deserted thing. Only the muffled clip-clop of horses' hoofs in the dust broke the silence.

Word of their coming had gone before them. As they reined in before Jumbo Jordan's place, a black-bearded man came to the doorway, a rifle gripped hard in hairy hands. The Cougar Kid recognised him. He went by the name of Swede Tyson. Behind him, in the shadows inside the so-called office, the Kid caught a glimpse of others he had mixed with during the brief period he had worked for Jumbo Jordan. They were a hard-bitten lot and if words became shots it wasn't at all certain that the ranchers would come off best.

Tyson eyed them sullenly.

'What goes on?' he demanded.

By general consent, Pete Farman seemed to be spokesman for the ranchers.

'We want to talk to Jordan,' he said. 'Where is he?'

'Dunno. Ain't seen him since yesterday.'

'You expectin' him back?'

Swede Tyson spat in the dust. Deliberately. Wiped his mouth with the back of a hairy hand; said:

'Sure we're expecting him back. He's responsible for the protection of this 'ere territory, ain't he?'

The ponderous sarcasm in his voice was obvious.

Pete Farman said: '*Was* responsible. From now on we're figuring to do our own protectin'.'

'Oh, yeah? And what do you figure Jumbo is gonna say about that when he gets back?'

Their eyes met, fought, battled it out unflinchingly. Swede Tyson may have been a rogue, but he was no coward.

Farman's hand dropped to the butt of his Colt.

'We don't care what he says. We've stood enough of it. He's poisoned our water-holes, run off our cattle. But this time he's gone too far. He's kidnapped Miss Bronson and that's one thing we ain't gonna stand for.'

Tyson brought his rifle up to his hip. His finger curled around the trigger.

'That's sure a pretty speech,' he said. 'So you ain't gonna stand for it? Now suppose you say what you *are* gonna do.'

Farman's horse reared a little. He steadied it with a practised hand.

'Just this, Tyson. We're gonna wreck this place and run you and your crowd outa town.'

'Think so.' Swede spat again in the red-brown dust. But he did so without once taking his eyes from Pete Farman. 'Now let me tell *you* what you're gonna do. First you're gonna turn over the Cougar Kid. He's one of Jumbo's men and I don't figure Jumbo would like to see him treated thataway.' His lazy drawl was suddenly lazy no longer. 'Cut him free, Farman. Quick. I've got a dozen gunslingers back in here backing me up.'

The muzzle of his rifle reared up, covering Farman's chest. There was a tinkling of breaking glass. Even as the glass clattered to the wooden sidewalk the barrels of two more rifles appeared where it had been.

Tyson said: 'I've got you covered, Farman. You an' all your crowd. There's a dozen guns trained on you and a dozen good men behind them. Now cut the Kid free.'

For a moment it looked as though Farman was going to obey. His hand came away from the butt of his gun. He half-turned in the saddle towards the Cougar Kid. Swede Tyson grinned in his beard.

But he grinned too soon.

Farman's hands gripped the reins of his sorrel. His spurs dug into its flanks. The animal reared. In the same instant Farman's hand wore a gun.

His voice rang loud and clear in the silent street.

'Scatter, boys, and let them have it. This is one time we ain't gonna be bluffed by a show of force. This is the show-down.'

And, suddenly, the silent street was

silent no longer. The roar of guns, the thud of hoofs, the shouts of men — all blended in a sudden outburst of hate and fury. A rifle shell sent Farman's hat spinning. Then he was on top of Swede Tyson, riding the actual sidewalk, his mount still plunging and rearing. Swede ducked; made a dive for the doorway. Too late. One of the sorrel's iron-shod hoofs caught him, sent him spinning. His rifle flew from his grasp. The others of Jumbo Jordan's outfit, behind the broken windows of the office, did their best to protect him, pouring shot after shot at Farman and his plunging mount.

But Farman was like a man gone berserk. Unflinchingly, with bullets screaming around him, he spurred the sorrel along the sidewalk to where Swede lay.

Swede saw him coming; rolled over; tried his damnedest to struggle to his feet.

The plunging hoofs of the sorrel caught him again as he tried to come up; knocked him down; battered him. From Swede Tyson's throat was torn a scream that was hardly human. Then he was silent, still, like a bundle of old clothes.

7

Someone cut the Cougar Kid loose from the black; dragged him from the saddle. He lay, his hands still tied, in the shadow of a narrow alleyway running between two of the woodframe shacks. He staggered to his feet, leaned back against the over-lapping boards. Beyond the alleyway, in Come Lucky's solitary street, it seemed all hell was let loose. Bullets kicked up the dust; men cursed and shouted as they pumped hot lead. The Kid saw Farman's sorrel go down under him; saw Farman himself, one arm swinging helplessly, blood dripping from his shoulder, run the gauntlet of a hail of bullets to dive for shelter behind a water-butt. Beside the Kid, a rancher was firing, reloading, firing again, until the barrels of his Colts must have been wellnigh red-hot. The stench of cordite was in the Kid's nostrils, a haze of gunsmoke before his eyes. To him it was meat and drink. His fingers itched for the feel of those white-butted Colts.

He dropped on one knee beside the rancher.

'Cut my hands loose; give me a gun. This is my fight, too.'

He meant it. Jumbo Jordan had led him up the garden and the Kid was never a man to stand for that. Somewhere, sometime, he was going to catch up with Jordan; settle accounts once and for all. In the meantime, the ranchers' fight was his fight.

But the man to whom he was speaking could not know that.

'What the hell do you take me for?' he tossed back over his shoulder as he worked the hammers of his guns. 'You're one of Jordan's men. By rights, I'd be doing everyone a good turn if I let you have yours.'

He turned, the idea crystallising inside him. The Cougar Kid saw that he meant it.

Like lightning, the Kid straightened up. His hands were tied still, but his feet were free. Even as the rancher began to rise the Kid kicked out. The pointed toe of his high-heeled riding boot took the man in the throat. He sprawled backwards, one of his guns flying from his grasp. Before he could recover the Kid was on him, kicking again . . . and again . . . and again. It wasn't pleasant, but the south-west in those days was not exactly a pleasant place. Men were inclined to shoot first and ask questions afterwards.

One of the Kid's kicks broke the rancher's nose. He staggered back; came to his knees with blood streaming from his face. He was clear of the alleyway; out in the bullet-riddled street. As the Kid kicked again he caught at his foot, jerked, twisted.

The Kid went sprawling on to the small of his back. The force of the fall knocked every last ounce of breath out of him. Through a purple haze as he struggled to force breath past the rattle in his throat he saw the rancher rise to his feet; saw the Colt in his hand rise with him. The snout of the Colt was a round, black, menacing hole.

But the hand that held it never tightened on the trigger. A stray bullet took the rancher in the back. He fell forward on his face in the dust.

The Kid lay half in, half out, of the alleyway. A bullet struck the heel of his boot. The shock jarred all the way up his leg. Still gasping for breath, he wriggled over on to his stomach, used his elbows to drag himself, Indian-fashion, back into the shadows where bullets could not reach.

Someone dropped on one knee beside him — Matt Bronson.

Bronson said:

'I must know where Jordan's taken my sister.'

He spoke crisply and quietly. The Kid, as he wriggled over again and staggered to his feet, realized that this was a new Matt Bronson. What had happened to his sister had jolted him out of himself; broken him clean of the shiftless life he had been leading. Never again would he be the pitiable object he had been that night in the Golden Nugget. The great south-west might be a hard, tough, lawless place, but it made men — if they had anything in them at all. It had made Matt Bronson.

The Kid hated lies. A liar, he always said, was worse than a horse-thief. A liar would hang his best friend.

But this was one time he had to lie.

He said: 'If I tell you where your sister is, do I get my guns and a chance to get clear?'

Bronson nodded.

'You do. Your guns are on your horse. It's tethered round back.'

The Kid nodded.

'OK, then. Cut these ropes.' He turned, extended his wrists, spoke over his shoulder. 'Jordan's taken your sister with him — '

He felt the ropes give as Bronson's knife slashed into them. He jerked his wrists and swung round in a single crisp movement.

Bronson said, eagerly: 'Yes — where?'

The Kid was smiling that cold, frosty smile of his.

'Sorry, Bronson, I don't know.'

Even as he said it his right hand was bunching and swinging up with all the power of a pile-driver.

Bronson had no time to avoid that vicious swing. The blow landed just where the Kid had intended it to land. A glazed look slid into Bronson's eyes and he crumpled like a half-empty sack of potatoes.

Even as he fell the Kid was jumping over him and sprinting down the short length of alleyway. At the end, round the turn, stood a bunch of cattle ponies. The big black stood a couple of hands above the rest of them. One of the Pete Farman crowd was with them. His hand went to his gun-butt and his eyes widened as he recognised the Kid.

'Hold it, feller. You ain't going no place.'

94

The Kid cursed himself inwardly for not having grabbed one of Bronson's guns. His own, if Bronson had been telling the truth, were with his horse. And a big black Colt, fast coming up to the ready position, was between him and the horse.

There was only one thing he could do — and he did it. Did it without thinking, acting on pure instinct and nothing else. He made straight for the Colt and the man who held it.

'You crazy loon,' yelled the man, and his thumb took back the hammer.

Without pause, the Kid swerved as he ran — swerved and dived bodily forward in a single lithe action that had a deal in common with the big mountain cat he was named after.

The Colt roared deafeningly in his ear — so near that the heat of the explosion scorched his face. Then his hand was gripping the barrel, jerking it up, and his leg was snaking round to sweep the other's legs from under him. The man sprawled in the red dust, but his grip on the Colt was a good one and it was still in his hand as the Kid charged into the bunch of cow-ponies. Another bullet fanned the Kid's cheek as he snatched the hitching rein free. He hit the black's rump, forked the saddle and gave the animal the merest touch of the spurs all in a single movement. The big black knew instinctively what was wanted of it.

The man belonging to the Pete Farman crowd was on his feet again, his Colt blasting, as the black went into a gallop. There was a yell from the Kid and he seemed to slide from the saddle. Instinctively, the rancher held his fire, waiting for the thud of a body hitting the dust. But nothing happened. The Kid, spread-eagled, Indian-fashion, along the far side of his horse, only the crook of one leg showing above the animal's body, grinned to himself. It was an old trick, but it had worked yet again. By the time the rancher realized what had happened he was out of gunshot, with the big black's hoofs fanning up dust in a way that looked as though there was no stopping the pair of them until they were clean over the State line into New Mexico.

But the Cougar Kid had no intention of doing anything of the sort. He still had an account to settle with Jumbo Jordan. And there was Gail Bronson to think of. She meant nothing to the Kid, but inside him, under his veneer of toughness, was an innate decency which refused to let him stand idly by while a nice kid like Gail Bronson was kidnapped and maltreated.

The only drawback was that he had no idea where Jordan had taken the girl. Comanche Bill would probably have known, But Comanche Bill was dead. The only others who might know were bottled up in that besieged office building on Come Lucky's main street. Well, there was only one answer to that.

Not until he was well clear of the town did the Kid swing his horse in a wide circle to bring it back towards

Come Lucky from another direction. As he rode he rummaged in his saddle-bag. The white-butted Colts were there. Not until they were back in the twin holsters lashed down to his thighs did he feel really comfortable.

The sound of gunfire from Come Lucky seemed more sporadic, less intense, as the Kid came within gunshot again. He reined in his horse on a piece of high ground and looked down on the place. Judging from the desultory puffs of smoke which preceded the sound of gunfire, the ranchers had got the office building pretty well surrounded. Some of them had clearly worked their way round to the open ground at the back to cut off any retreat on the part of Jumbo Jordan's crowd.

The Kid sighed. It wasn't going to be easy.

He cantered his horse along the river valley from which Come Lucky drew its water supply. Where the valley ended he left the black in a clump of willows — he had no fear that it would stray

— and crawled cautiously up the incline. Flat on his stomach, he studied the position. There were a clear thirty yards of open ground between himself and the nearest building. It was a risk, but it had to be taken.

He waited until there was another outburst of firing to occupy the attention of both besiegers and besieged, then ran, doubled up, across the short stretch of open country to throw himself flat on the rear veranda of the nearest shack. No bullets came his way. Cautiously, carefully, with all the skill of an Indian tracker, he made his way from building to building along the whole length of the street.

Then he could go no further. Ahead of him, crouched in the angle of the next building, were two of Pete Farman's party. Their backs were to him, their attention concentrated on the building beyond, where the rest of the Jumbo Jordan crowd were at bay. But obviously it was impossible to get past them.

The Cougar Kid lay flat in the dust, perfectly motionless. Only his head moved as he turned it carefully from side to side. The sound of gunfire told him there was someone else round the corner of the building to his right. To the left was open ground, with not a vestige of shade or cover as far as the eye could see. Beside him was a water-butt.

Cautiously, he straightened up, his eyes never leaving the backs of the two ranchers crouched down ahead of him. Then, judging his moment, he swung himself up on to the water-butt, extended his arms, let his fingers hook over the edge of the roof . . . a jump and a jerk and he was up.

The roof had a slope of sorts, but nothing to worry about. Flat on his face, the Kid edged his way along. He came to the end; peered over the edge. Below him were the two ranchers. Had either of the two looked up at that moment they must have seen him. But their gaze was concentrated in another direction.

There was a gap of four feet between him and the next building, a flat-roofed shack. Beyond that, with another gap of four feet separating the two, was the building in which Dutch Henry was barricaded.

The Kid worked his way back from the edge; came into a crouching position. Suddenly he straightened up; ran — awkwardly because of the slope of the roof; hurled himself forward.

There was a yell and a shot. Then his feet were on the flat roof of the next building and he was running, crouched. His very life depending upon it. But the element of surprise was with him.

It took those surrounding the building perhaps two seconds after that first yell and shot to appreciate what was happening. But in those two seconds the Kid had covered the length of the roof and was hurtling through the air a second time. As he jumped he wore those white-butted guns of his in his hands.

He landed, surefooted as a mountain

cat, just as a fusillade of shots burst around him. The shooting was wild, hurried.

Ahead the Kid saw the glass skylight he knew was there. Two more paces brought him to it. The heel of his riding boot jabbed at it, quickly, fiercely. Glass shattered. Then the Kid, guns in hands, dropped bodily through the opening.

8

There was a table immediately beneath the sky-light. The Cougar Kid landed squarely on it with a thud, guns searching the smoke-filled room. The table shuddered under the jar, tilted, and two of the legs gave way with a harsh rending sound.

The long, low room was a haze of gunsmoke. There were eleven men in it and five of them were dead. The other six swung round as one man as the Kid thudded into the room.

Dutch Henry, a smoking six-gun in either hand, grinned through his beard.

'Well, if it ain't the Cougar Kid, turned up to give his mates a helping hand. Thought you was all set for the high jump, Kid, the way they had you hogtied to that horse.'

The remark left an opening for a clever man to pretend he had come in friendship, to fight alongside Dutch and the others while he ferreted out what he had come to learn. But the Cougar Kid was seldom subtle. He knew only one method of getting what he wanted ... a direct, straight-forward, honest-to-God method with no fancy tricks and no holds barred. The guns in his hands made a threatening gesture.

'I'm not here to give anyone a helping hand. I'm here to square accounts with Jumbo. Where is he?'

Dutch Henry's eyes narrowed. 'You heard what Swede told that crowd ... ' He broke off to flick a lightning shot through the broken window in the direction of a head careless enough to show itself round a corner ... 'out thyar. We don't know. Ain't seen him since he went out with you and Comanche last night.'

The Kid said: 'Where would he be likely to go?'

There was a rattle of shots from outside. Those inside busied themselves replying. The haze of gunsmoke thickened. Dutch Henry shifted his chewing-tobacco from one cheek to another.

'Depends upon what he had in mind.'

The Kid said, curtly: 'He had Gail Bronson in mind.'

'In that case, I reckon — ' Dutch Henry broke off abruptly, a crafty look in his eyes. 'I've told you once — I don't know where in the hell Jumbo is.'

'You may not know, but you could make a pretty good guess,' hazarded the Kid.

'What if I could?'

The Kid's eyes were like granite chippings; his words like slivers of pure ice.

'Tell me what I want to know, Dutch, or these guns start talking.'

Dutch's bearded mouth curled in a sneer. 'We're six to one, Kid. You may be good, but you ain't that good.'

'We'll see. You've got six seconds, Dutch, so start talking. One, two, three, four — '

That was as far as the Kid got. Maybe he saw Slim Dakars out of the corner of his eye. Maybe he sensed him; did what he did on pure instinct.

Dakars was crouching by the window, looking out, firing whenever there was something to fire at. But now he brought his right gun up under his left armpit; started to turn; fired as he turned.

The Kid sprang aside, his own guns blasting. The wood-built office rocked with gunfire, with the Kid pumping shots faster than the other six put together. Anyone who didn't see it would have said that it was downright impossible. They were gunslingers, those six, but none of them had that uncanny speed of the Cougar Kid. When the frenzied gunplay was over Slim Dakars was still crouching beneath the window. But it was the huddled crouch of a dead man. Another man sprawled across the broken remnants of the table with glazing eyes. Rod Repton sat dazedly in a corner, trying to staunch the blood flowing from a gaping wound the Kid's shells had punched in his stomach. Dutch Henry stood, cursing, looking down at two broken hands — the trademark of those who crossed the Cougar Kid and lived to tell the tale. The other two had the ashen faces of men who have looked on death.

'Drop those guns,' from the Kid.

They did as he said, while Dutch Henry cursed them for their cowardice.

The Kid himself had not come through the affair untouched. Blood stained his shirt where a shell had raked his ribs. There was more blood higher up where another shell had gone clean through the fleshy part of the forearm. He swayed slightly on his feet. But the guns in his hands were rock-steady.

'You an' me's going places, Dutch,' he said. 'You're going to take me to where Jordan's holing out.'

Dutch looked down at his mangled hands.

'Like heck I am,' he snarled. 'My life wouldn't be worth two bits if I did. Jordan would flay me.'

'Your life isn't worth two bits if you

don't,' said the Kid, levelly. He gestured with one of his guns. 'Get over here.'

Dutch Henry did as he was told, but not without protest.

'You're plumb loco,' he said. 'Even if I did know where Jordan was, there ain't no way of getting out of here. Those fools out there have got the place surrounded.'

'We'll see about that. You — ' The Kid's gun jerked towards one of the two gunslingers who were still unharmed. 'Take off your neckerchief.'

With a surprised look on his face, the man did as he was told.

'Tie it to that rifle.' The Kid stood where he could watch the whole crowd at once. 'That's right. Now stick it out of the window.'

The man's face hardened. 'Not me. I'm not waving no surrender flag. Those guys will lynch us once they get their mitts on us.'

The Kid smiled that frosty smile of his.

'That's a chance you have to take. If

you don't do it, I'll shoot you where you stand.'

Dutch Henry said: 'You wouldn't shoot an unarmed man.'

'Wouldn't I?' There was an ominous click as the Kid took back the hammer.

Maybe he was bluffing — though there are those who say that the Kid never bluffed. Maybe he would have gone through with it, for his fighting blood was up and he was ready to go through hell and high water to settle accounts with Jumbo Jordan. But whether he was bluffing or not will never be known. The man's nerve gave.

'Don't shoot. I'll do it.'

He flattened himself against the wooden wall and cautiously thrust the barrel of the rifle through the broken window. A bullet whipped the dirty silk neckerchief fluttering at the end. Outside someone shouted: 'Hold your fire, boys. They're willing to talk turkey.'

A great quiet descended on the dusty, sunbaked street.

The Kid said: 'Tell them you're coming out.'

The gunslinger did so.

A breathing space of maybe ten seconds; then Pete Farman's voice said: 'OK. Only keep your hands up and don't try anything.'

The Kid tossed a glance through the rear window. A man, rifle in hand, was scuttling across the open space beyond. He disappeared beyond the angle of the Kid's vision. The Kid smiled quietly. It was working as he had hoped it would work. The act of surrender was focusing attention on the front of the building.

One of his guns jabbed into Dutch Henry's ribs.

'Get over by that rear door. When these two go out front you go out back. I'll be right behind you.' He turned to the other two. 'Get going. Take Repton with you. He needs a doc bad.'

Rod Repton yelled with pain as the other two picked him up. They cast a hesitating glance backwards at the Cougar Kid.

'Get going,' he said.

The guns in his hands brooked no further argument. The foremost of the two kicked open the door with his foot; hesitated a moment more; then the two went out, carrying the injured man between them. The hush outside was broken by a fierce yell from the ranchers.

Dutch looked at the Kid with baleful eyes.

'You ain't human,' he said. 'If there's anyone out there, I'll get it as sure as God made little apples.'

There was a curious look in the Kid's hard, cold eyes.

'Think I haven't thought of that,' he said. 'Out you go.'

Dutch looked at the Kid; looked at those levelled guns. He turned towards the door. The Kid took down the latch; threw the door open. It swung idly in the breeze. No shot came.

Dutch stepped outside, the Kid following. His gun gestured. 'Along there. Keep close to the buildings. Walk

111

quickly, but don't panic. Act as though you've got a perfect right to be doing what you're doing.'

Dutch had no option but to obey. With the Kid close behind, he sneaked along in the rear of the buildings. No one saw them. Everyone's attention was concentrated on what was happening at the front.

The Kid said: 'This hide-out of Jumbo's — where is it?'

Dutch said: 'In the Sierras. An old Indian cave settlement. I've been there once. I think I might find it again. On your own, you might hunt for a hundred years and never locate it.'

He could have been lying to save his own skin, but the Kid didn't think so. Dutch Henry, his hands shot to pieces, was a broken man. The way he spoke had the ring of truth about it. Besides, the Kid knew the Sierras — if any man could be said to know that vast mountain wilderness of mighty crags and yawning chasms. He knew it was true, indeed, that you might hunt a hundred years and never find the place you were seeking. It was a maze of mountain crags in which a man might lose himself forever, to die of thirst and end up a heap of mouldering bones.

'You'll need a horse,' he said.

Dutch nodded.

They had come to the end of the buildings. Ahead lay the river valley where the Kid had left his big rawboned black. Beyond the river the open country, rising and falling in great folds. Beyond the prairie, the Sierras.

Around the turn a group of horses were hitched to a rail. The Kid halted.

'Go get one,' he said.

Dutch looked down at his broken and bloody hands.

'Someone might see me,' he said. 'If they do, I can't do a thing about it.'

'That's a chance you have to take,' said the Kid, curtly. 'I'll be covering you.'

Normally, he would have thought twice about taking another man's horse. Horse-stealing was a capital crime in the southwest. You could shoot another man down, and, provided you did it in fair gunplay, no one would bat an eyelid. But to steal another man's horse was asking to be stretched at the end of a limb.

But the Kid, that day, was beyond such scruples. Inside him, something was tying itself in knots until it lay like a hard ball in the pit of his stomach . . . a ball that would disappear only when he had settled accounts with Jumbo Jordan.

He leaned negligently against the corner of the building and watched Dutch walk towards the cluster of cow-ponies. Dutch's broken hands made even unhitching a difficult and lengthy operation. But he managed it in the end. Somehow he swung himself into the saddle. From where the Kid stood he could see the look of anguish on the other's face as he forced himself to use those blood-smeared fingers.

A cowpuncher came strolling round the far corner of the building. The Kid did not appear to change his negligent attitude one jot, but inside he was suddenly poised and tense.

A look of surprise came over the cowpuncher's face as he saw Dutch swinging himself into the saddle of a piebald; surprise which changed to fury.

His mouth opened in an angry shout.

'Hi, there. You. Get off — '

Even as he yelled his right hand was going for his gun. But the Kid was faster. Very much faster.

Even as the gun came out of its holster a shell from one of the Kid's guns whammed into it. It was very pretty shooting. The cowpuncher's gun went flying while the cowpuncher himself nursed numbed fingers.

Then the Cougar Kid was swinging himself up behind Dutch Henry, jabbing his spurs into the flanks of the piebald, urging it towards the river valley. He flung himself off as they skidded down the moist grassy slope towards the clump of willows. A whistle came from between his teeth. Obediently the big black came trotting out. The Kid swung himself into the saddle.

The two of them came up over the ridge at a gallop, the big black's legs flexing and unflexing in a long raking tireless stride that could go on for hours. Dutch Henry, somehow nursing the reins of the piebald in his crippled hands, flung a glance behind them. An oath left his bearded lips.

The Kid looked back as he rode. Behind them, issuing from the solitary main street of Come Lucky, was a bunch of horsemen. He counted eight of them. They fanned out into a semi-circle as they rode. There was no doubt as to their intention.

'Seems like your pals have tipped them off to us,' the Kid said.

He had expected as much. But he had hoped that in the excitement of surrender no one would pay much heed to the gunslingers' protests that two of their number had sneaked out through the rear exit. Evidently someone had, and now there was a posse of irate ranchers on their tail. It wasn't going to help matters. He settled down to some long, hard riding.

9

As dawn broke over the Sierras, at the time the Cougar Kid had waited beneath that cottonwood tree with a noose about his neck and the Farman crowd around him, Gail Bronson stirred into consciousness. Her body jolted and jarred painfully as the horse across which she was thrown picked its way carefully over the rough, uneven ground.

Jumbo Jordan walked ahead, holding the hitching rein. Anything faster than walking pace was out of question in that rocky territory of narrow trails, sheer drops and razor-sharp ridges. As the sun rose higher, beating down fiercely on the red, jagged rocks, they came to a defile where the rock face rose sheer on either side like skyscrapers flanking a city street. Beyond the defile the trail sloped sharply down again into the very heart of the Sierras. It was a wild, uncharted, rocky wilderness.

Then, suddenly, its character changed. They entered a wide valley where the trail ran alongside a mountain stream. Trees shaded the stream and grass grew beside it. Beyond the stream another rock-face of red sandstone seemingly rose sheer to the sky. Jordan led the horse across the stream and straight towards the rock face. High up — so high that you had to crane your neck to see — openings were cut in the rock, mountain caves where Indians had once dwelt.

There are many such cave dwellings in the Sierras, dating back to long before the white man trekked west. Jordan had found this particular deserted village when exploring the Sierras soon after he first arrived in Come Lucky. The caves and the valley had since served him in good stead. Cattle rustled from ranches which did not join the so-called Protection Association had found their way to the valley; had cropped there while a running iron did its work on their brands.

Kidnapped ranchers, blindfolded so that they did not know their whereabouts, had been held prisoner in those cliff-face caves until they had decided to toe the line. Wanted men had hidden out there; stolen gold had been stored there.

Jordan halted the horse at the foot of the rock face; grinned as he saw that Gail had recovered consciousness. She shrank away from him as he lifted her down from the horse.

Jumbo snorted.

'Finicky little filly, ain't you? Maybe you won't be so finicky when I'm through with you.'

The girl looked at him defiantly.

'You must be mad,' she said. 'You won't get away with this.'

Jumbo laughed — a deep, throaty laugh.

'Think not?' he said. 'Then think again. Nobody knows where you are. Nobody's gonna come looking for you. For all anyone knows, you were burnt to death in the ranch-house.'

Gail said: 'They'll connect you with that.'

'Maybe. They connect me with a lot of things. But they're never able to prove it. It wouldn't get them any place if they could. I'm the boss around these parts.'

'Think so? Then let me tell you something. Know where my brother was last night? He was over at Pete Farman's place. With a whole lot of others — working out how they could settle with you.'

She hadn't meant to tell him, but hate and rage and fear had gotten the better of discretion.

Jumbo shrugged.

'They won't do anything. They've met before — a score of times. It doesn't get them any place. Know why?' He thrust his face close to hers. 'Because there ain't a real man among the lot of them. You should be pleased you've got yourself a real man at last, girlie.'

121

'Call yourself a man,' the girl sneered. 'Pete Farman's twice the man you are.'

Jordan hitched at his gunbelts.

'We'll see about that. Once you're safely tucked away I think me and Pete Farman's gonna have a reckoning. Seems to me he's at the bottom of all this trouble I've been having.'

He looked up at the rock face and whistled twice on a rising and falling note. Presently a roughly fashioned rope ladder came tumbling down. Jordan motioned Gail towards it.

'Start climbin'.'

Gail put her hands on the ladder and started to climb. It swayed sickeningly as she went up. A jerk on the ladder told her that Jordan was climbing up after her. The wind whistled around her as she climbed higher. She came to the first of the cave-like entrances.

'In you go,' Jordan shouted from below.

Gail climbed into the cave. Outside she heard Jordan shouting to someone.

Then he climbed in after her. It was cold in the cave, gloomy with it.

Jordan said: 'Croota will be here in a moment. She's going to look after you for me. You'll like Croota.' But the tone of his voice didn't go along with the words.

Over his shoulder Gail saw the flimsy ladder sway and shudder as someone else set foot on it.

She was incredibly old, incredibly ugly, the Indian squaw who stepped from the ladder to shuffle towards them across the cave. Her mouth was a dark opening of yellow, toothless gums. Her fingernails were long, dirty claws; her nose hooked like a vulture's. Her face was a criss-cross network of wrinkles. When she opened her mouth only strange, animal-like grunts emerged.

Jordan said: 'Croota is dumb. Her tongue was cut out a long time ago. Things might have been very much worse, but I saved her from that. Now she does anything I say. She will look after you till I get back from settling with Pete Farman.'

Hope sprang into the girl's eyes. Jordan must have seen it, for he said:

'You won't get away. There won't be any ladder. Croota lives in the cave above. She will pull the ladder up again once I have gone.'

He looked at the old crone who wagged her head in frantic comprehension.

Gail felt suddenly frightened. But she was determined that neither Jordan nor the Indian woman should see how she felt. She sat on a ledge of rock to hide the sudden trembling of her limbs.

Jordan said, chuckling: 'Take good care of her, Croota.' Then he swung himself on to the ladder and disappeared from view.

The Indian stood looking down at the girl, still making hideous cackling noises, a half-crazy look in her sunken eyes. She reached out and touched the smooth skin of the girl's arm with those claw-like fingers. Gail jerked her arm away. From below in the valley came the distant sound of hoofs marking Jordan's departure. The Indian shuffled away towards the entrance of the cave.

It was then that Gail sprang at her.

The girl's attack was a move of sheer desperation. Even should she succeed in getting clear of the cave, on foot, without a horse, with no knowledge of the myriad rocky trails of the Sierras, she stood little chance of finding her way out to the open rangeland again. But she gave no thought to that. All that she knew was that she had to get away before Jumbo Jordan returned.

She grabbed the dirty blanket which draped the old woman and tried to throw it over her head. But if she had thought to find Croota an easy victim, she was speedily disillusioned. Nails that were like knives bit into the bare flesh of her arms, drawing blood, leaving long weals behind them.

Years of hard living had toughened the old Indian woman, made her muscles like whipcord. The two of them crashed, struggling, to the rocky floor of the cave. Gail's hands fought for a hold on the old woman's dirty, multitudinous clothes. The rancid stench of the Indian's body was in her nostrils. Nails clawed at the gingham frock, ripping it. Then those claw-like hands were about Gail's throat, choking her, forcing her head back.

Desperately she writhed, this way and that, seeking to shake them loose, seeking to gulp fresh air into her lungs. Her fists pounded the old woman's toothless face. The mouth opened in a distorted grin and horrible cackling sounds came out.

Gail grabbed at one of the skinny wrists, struggling to wrench it free of her throat. Then she was underneath the old woman and hard, bony knees were pinning her slim, young body to the rocky ground. Her hand threshed at her side, encountered something; her fingers gripped it.

Scarcely knowing what she did, Gail smashed the broken piece of rock sideways against the old woman's head.

Again and again. And suddenly there was no weight on her chest any more, no clawlike hands locked about her throat. Panting, struggling for breath, she staggered to her feet. Her breast was heaving; her throat felt stiff and sore. The gingham frock was ripped all down one side.

The old Indian woman lay in a crumpled heap, making little moaning sounds to herself. But her eyes, fixed on Gail, were still black and beady. Suddenly her hand whipped beneath the blanket which hung around her. A knife glittered in the gloom of the cave when the hand emerged again. She began to crawl towards the girl, one leg dragging behind her as though it was broken.

Turning, the girl rushed towards the cave entrance. Desperately she groped for the rope ladder; swung herself on to it. Looking back, she saw the old woman, knife in hand, dragging herself across the floor of the cave, making meaningless sounds to herself as she came on.

Rapidly Gail began to climb down the rope ladder. Her foot slipped and for a brief instant she hung by her hands. She got her foot back on to the ladder and went on climbing down, her whole body trembling.

Suddenly there came a jerk which almost pitched her from the ladder. The rough rope, rushing through her fingers, seared the flesh. She steadied herself and looked up. The old woman was leaning out of the cave entrance, hanging on to the ladder with one hand. The other hand held the knife. And below the flashing blade Gail saw that one of the ropes which formed the ladder had been completely severed.

The cutting of the rope had rendered the wooden struts which formed the rungs of the ladder well-nigh useless. They hung down at a drunken angle. And now the knife was at work on the single rope that remained. Gail felt the rawhide give under her weight as the blade bit through the first few strands.

She looked down. The floor of the

canyon still seemed a long way off. She shuddered as she looked at the jagged rocks below and felt beads of cold sweat break out on her forehead. Hurriedly she began to descend the rest of the ladder, her feet hanging loose, the rawhide rushing through her fingers with excruciating agony.

It gave again under her weight as more strands were severed, pitching her bodily against the rock wall. Her senses reeled, but she knew she had to keep going down. To get as near the bottom as she could before the knife cut through the remaining rope altogether.

Then it happened. The fall jolted every last ounce of air from her body. Gasping for breath, she half-staggered, half-crawled, across the floor of the canyon to the soft green grass and the shelter of the trees. She dragged herself to where the stream babbled over boulders, forced her hands to splash the cool, clear water over her face and body. She looked at her hands. They were a mass of raw flesh. The gingham frock was in ribbons. Overhead, beyond the shadow of the trees, the sun blazed down.

She began to walk. She knew which way Jordan had brought her into the valley and that was the way she headed. The going was easy enough while there was grass underfoot, but once that had been left behind, once the murmur of the stream had faded, once there was only rock underfoot as the trail sloped sharply upwards, she began to realize what she had let herself in for.

She came to a part where the trail — if you could call it a trail — forked. All around the jagged rocks lifted their probing fingers to the hot sky. She tried to climb one to see if she could locate her whereabouts, but the sheer smooth surface of rock make it impossible. She tried to remember which way she had travelled with Jordan. But it was no use. One fork seemed as likely as the other.

On and on. On and on. The rough surface underfoot tore her shoes to shreds. Sweat ran down her body; soaked her clothing. Her whole body ached intolerably. Desperately she forced herself to continue putting one tired leg before the other.

The rocks around her seemed to shimmer in the heat-haze, swaying and agitating like living things. She had to put her hand on one to convince herself that it was really still. And it came as no surprise to find that she could not keep the hand from trembling. Her mouth felt hot and parched; her tongue swollen. She thought of that cool, clear stream which had murmured its way through the valley, and the thought was additional torment.

She fell down, forced herself to her feet, struggled on. Vaguely, she was aware of falling again; of going on on hands and knees, forcing her limbs to do things beyond their capabilities. The rock surface of the trail was burning hot to her touch, tormenting to her raw hands. The agony of it jerked her back to full realisation. She tried to get to her feet, but the effort was beyond her.

In her ear a far-off voice murmured: 'Keep a-going. Keep a-going.' Vaguely, she realized that it was her own voice. It went on a long time, babbling meaningless things.

The sun began to descend the western sky. The rock fingers threw long shadows. Afterwards, Gail didn't remember crawling half-conscious into the coolness those shadows offered, and lying there while purple gathered over the hills.

She imagined she could hear the murmur of the stream again, cleaving its way over the rocks; the rush of cold air down the canyon as she climbed that swaying rope ladder with Jumbo Jordan behind her. She imagined she could hear the sound of steel-shod hoofs striking loose shale; feel the coolness of the stream on her raw-red hands. She was drinking at the stream. Only it wasn't water. It was raw whiskey, making her choke and gasp.

She sat up, choking. It *was* whiskey. The rawness of it bit into her tired limbs. She struggled to her feet, hope and joy bounding inside her. Purple twilight, the forerunner of night, hung between the mighty crags. She put out a hand, pushing the proffered whiskey flask away from her.

'Thanks — that's enough,' she gasped.

Only then did she look up for the first time. Straight into the fat, heavy-jowled face of Jumbo Jordan.

10

Jumbo Jordan, when he had left the girl at the cave, had headed back rapidly the way he had come — or as rapidly as the tricky nature of those winding mountain trails would permit. He was no fool and he knew that he had let impulse outrun reason, let lust outweigh common sense. It had been the act of an idiot to kidnap Gail Bronson without making quite sure that there was no one left alive who might put the finger on him. That, of course, was the way it would have been but for the intervention of the Cougar Kid.

Well, it was no good crying over spilt milk. If anyone was alive to put the finger on him, he could always bluff his way out as he had done many times in the past. If he couldn't bluff his way out, he could always shoot his way out. As for the girl's talk about Pete Farman and the others ... He snorted and snapped his fingers as he rode. Let them try something. Let them just try. They'd soon learn who was king of the range in this territory ... if the destruction of the Crazy Y hadn't been lesson enough. Before Jumbo Jordan was through with them, they'd pay up and like it.

His eye, as the trail came out at a point which overlooked the vast rangeland, travelled to that distant dustcloud on the horizon where the roundup was still in progress. Eighteen thousand head of beef there'd be in that herd when it started the long trek up the Chisholm Trail to be sold at the railhead in Dodge City. That was eighteen thousand dollars to be collected in protection money. He rubbed his big hands together at the thought. They'd pay all right. Knowing Jumbo Jordan, they'd stump up, every man-jack of 'em, rather than take the risk of anything happening to a herd that size.

His eyes narrowed suddenly as they

focused on another, smaller, dustcloud nearer to hand — a dust-cloud that moved, forming a curve like the slender sickle of a new moon. Ahead of the dustcloud were two tiny fleeing dots. At that distance they were no more than that — two tiny black shapeless blobs — but Jordan, his eyes accustomed to the endless distances of the open rangeland, knew that the blobs were two horsemen. Horsemen heading for the broken ridges of the Sierras as though all hell was at their heels. And the dustcloud behind them represented other horsemen, a posse of them, the actual riders obscured by the dust their mounts kicked up, galloping hell for leather in pursuit. He sat his saddle, wondering what it added up to.

Below him the tiny blob that was the Cougar Kid, high-tailing it across the rangeland, turned in his saddle — though he was too far off for Jordan to know what he did. He looked back at the pursuing posse. The distance which separated them was exactly what it had been a couple of miles back. No more and no less. He slackened rein and let the big black ease up a trifle.

Dutch Henry turned and looked at him. 'You aiming for them to catch up with us?' he said suspiciously.

The Kid shook his head.

'If my hunch is right, they won't.'

His hunch was right. Ten minutes later he looked back again. The distance was still the same. So the posse had slackened rein, too. That looked as though they weren't in any hurry to catch up. The Kid thought he knew the answer to that one. Those in the posse were quite content to sit quietly on their tails in the hope that they would be led straight to Jumbo Jordan and Gail Bronson.

The ground began to rise. They were in the foothills. The big rawboned black bounded uphill with powerful thrusts of those mighty back legs.

'See those two peaks.' Dutch pointed with a maimed hand to where twin pinnacles of rock rose like sentinels above the first range of crags. 'We make for those. There's a trail runs between them.'

The Kid nodded. 'First though we've got to throw this bunch of our tail.'

He had no desire to go after Jumbo Jordan with a posse on his tail. What was between him and Jumbo was a strictly personal thing. He wanted no outside intervention.

Their horses crested the rise. The Kid looked back. Behind them the posse was beginning to close in a little now that the ground was becoming broken and rugged. The Kid gentled the black forward until he judged the crest hid them from view. Then he grabbed the rein of Dutch's pinto and swung both horses sharply to the left.

'Like the wind,' he said. 'This is where we lose them.'

Old in the art of trailing and being trailed, the Kid had picked his spot well. The rise and fall of the ground, with each rise slightly higher than the one before, formed a series of shallow valleys running parallel with the mountain range. It was along the first of these valleys that the Kid and his unwilling companion rode with every ounce of speed they could urge from their mounts. Ahead an outcrop of red rock jutted out into the grassy valley. Once round that and they would be screened from view.

It worked just as the Kid had hoped it would. Pete Farman and his crowd, topping the rise, coasted downhill and began to climb again. They could no longer see the two men they had been pursuing, but it never occurred to any one of them that they were not still ahead — just beyond the next rise, and, when that was reached, beyond the rise after that.

The Kid, once the outcrop of rock hid him and Dutch from view, slid from the black's back and hurriedly scaled the nearest rock-face. From the top, flattened out, he saw Farman and his crowd go tearing straight on. The rise hid them from view in turn, but the Kid was too wily a hand to let that assume anything for him. Patiently he waited until he saw them silhouetted against the rise after that and the one after that. Judging by the dustcloud that hung in their rear, they were still going strong. Contented, he dangled his legs over the edge of the rock and began to ease himself to the ground.

He had forgotten that Dutch Henry was not with him of his own free will and accord. He was halfway down when the clatter of hoofs reached his ears. Clinging precariously to the rock face, he turned his head. Dutch Henry, his broken hands now roughly bandaged with strips of his torn neckerchief, was making off into the hills. And he was taking the Kid's big black with him, the hitching rein of the black looped round the saddle-horn of the piebald. But he wasn't having an easy job of it. The black, a one-man horse, was plunging and rearing, jerking at the length of hitching rein, trying its damnedest to tear itself free.

Hurriedly the Kid scrambled down the remainder of the rock face, tearing his buckskin chaps in the process. His hands went to his guns, but he knew that he was wasting his time. Despite the frantic resistance of the black, Dutch Henry was already out of gunshot, urging the piebald forward along a narrow ledge of rock which wound into the hills. A rifle would have done the trick, but the Kid's rifle was in the black's saddle-scabbard.

He began to run forward across the uneven ground, but even as he did so he knew that it was useless. Slow as Dutch Henry was progressing because of the tricky nature of the trail, he was moving a heck of a sight faster than a man could hope to move on foot.

The Kid stood stockstill and let out that peculiar whistle of his. The echo of it came back to him from the rocky crags. The black heard it and redoubled its efforts to free itself. All the fury of its mustang predecessors came uppermost. Snorting, it hurled itself at the pinto.

The pinto staggered, whinnying with terror. Dutch cursed. Though it must have hurt his broken hand like hell, he seized the quirt which hung from the pinto's saddle and used it to lash at the black's nose.

But the black was a throw-back to those wild mustangs which have been known to mix it with a mountain lion and come out best. It reared as far as the hitching rein would permit, flailing the air with furious hoofs. Dutch did the only thing he could do. Rapidly he untwined the hitching rein and urged the pinto forward out of reach. The Kid whistled again. The black paused in its rearing, ears twitching. Then it turned. Its hind legs went over the edge of the trail, scrabbling furiously at the sloping rock below as it struggled to recover its balance. Then it was up and flying back along the trail to where the Cougar Kid waited.

Cow-ponies are the mongrels of the equine world. And the black was a mongrel even among mongrels. But it was trembling like a nervous thoroughbred as it halted where the Kid waited. 'Good boy. There's a feller,' he said, patting its quivering neck as he swung himself into the saddle. He swung the black round and raked it gently with his spurs, taking the same trail that Dutch had taken.

*   *   *

Jumbo Jordan, from the mountain eyrie where he sat his horse, had seen only part of all this. He had seen those two flying dots crest the distant rise and then swing sideways along the valley to disappear behind an outcrop which hid them from his view; he had seen the pursuing dustcloud carry straight on and had grinned to himself in appreciation of the trick. He had waited until the dustcloud was lost to view round the distant edge of the bluff and had then ridden on, easing his mount carefully down the steep, narrow trail. He rode with his hand on his gun.

Somewhere ahead of him were the two riders who had been just fleeing blobs when he last saw them. He might never see them again in that tangled labyrinth of rock and stone. He might, equally, round any rock face to find himself suddenly face to face with them. He was taking no chances.

Suddenly there was the clatter of hoofs on rock. Jordan jerked his horse to a standstill, backed up a little. His gun was out in his hand. Round the bend, its flanks heaving, its painted body awash with sweat, its hind feet slipping and slithering in the loose shale, came the piebald. Dutch Henry was crouching in the saddle, one arm flung around the horn to lessen the anguish which came from broken hands gripping the reins.

He was on top of Jumbo almost before he saw him, jerking the piebald frantically to a standstill. The terrified look on his bearded face eased as he saw who it was.

'Blast you, Jumbo,' he said, 'where in

the hell have you been? All hell's let loose back there. Pete Farman an' his crowd came stompin' into town out for blood. They've bust up the office and croaked most of the boys. The Cougar Kid gave them a hand with that — '

'The Cougar Kid!'

Hate and fury blazed in Jordan's eyes.

'Sure thing. He's high-tailin' me now. He's sure out to get you, Jumbo, and he was makin' me lead him to you. Only I gave him the slip back there — ' He broke off as the distant rattle of hoofs came floating to them on the quiet air.

Dutch said: 'That's him — the swine.'

'Get a grip on yourself,' said Jumbo, roughly. 'There's two of us to one of him. He's only a man like the rest of us.'

'A man! He's not a man — he's a devil!' Dutch held up his bandaged hands. 'That's what he's done to me — crippled me. I'll never shoot again. Never!'

'Cut it out, you fool,' snarled Jumbo. 'I'm not scared of the Cougar Kid if you are. And I'm not beaten yet. Bust things up for me, have they? I'll square with them for that.' He jerked his hand up along the trail. 'Keep going, Dutch. I want that coyote to hear you. He'll get suspicious if he don't hear anything.'

'But — '

'You heard me. Git.'

Dutch did as he was told, pricking the pinto into a canter, its hoofs echoing dully on the hard rock. Jumbo watched him go, then swung his own horse round and urged it clear of the trail into a narrow crevasse which ran between the rocks. He swung down from the saddle, took his lariat from the saddle horn and began to climb.

The Cougar Kid rode on steadily, climbing higher and ever higher into the lonely Sierras, pausing once in awhile to listen for the sound of Dutch's horse ahead. Sometimes, by a trick of sound among the lofty peaks, he heard the hoofs of the pinto loud and clear, almost as though it was jogging along only a length or so ahead; sometimes he heard them only muffled and distant; sometimes he didn't hear them at all. But he knew that Dutch was somewhere ahead of him; knew that in the end, if only because he had no other place to go now, he had to lead him to Jumbo Jordan's hide-out.

His lean face hardened at the thought. Suddenly his black stopped of its own accord, trembling, sniffing the wind. The Kid and his horse had been together too long for him not to know that the animal, with its acute sense of smell, its natural awareness of danger, had sensed something of which he, himself, was not yet aware. He leaned forward, peering along the trail. It curved round and up — empty. The clatter of hoofs came faintly to his ears. That would be Dutch Henry's pinto, still a fair way ahead. Yet danger was close at hand. The black's awareness, communicating itself to him in some strange way that only those of the great open spaces know, told him that. Well, there was only one way to find out what the danger was and in which direction it lay.

His right hand went to the butt of one of those long-barrelled .45 Colts he wore. The other gave a gentle shake to the reins. With seeming reluctance, the black cantered forward again.

Then it happened. There was a gentle swish in the air. A raw-hide noose snaked neatly around the Kid's head, dropped over his shoulders, jerked tight. His hand was snatched from the butt of the Colt and pinioned to his body as he was jerked from the saddle to crash to the hard rocky surface of the trail.

There was a coarse laugh, a slither of feet. A gun-butt thudded on the Kid's head as he struggled to get up. Then, as he fought his reeling senses, a hog-string was whipped around his wrists and pulled tight: it was a long time since Jumbo Jordan had ridden the range as an ordinary cowhand, but he was far from forgetting the tricks of the trade.

He jerked the Kid roughly to his feet. 'Planning to catch up with me, were you?' he snarled. 'Well, you've got your wish.'

His hand lashed the Kid across the mouth, splitting his lip. He took the blow unflinchingly, savouring the salt taste of blood in his mouth.

'OK,' he said. 'Get it over with.'

'Oh, no.' Jordan shook his great head, his mass of hair flopping over his forehead. 'For you it ain't gonna be so easy as that. I've got plans for you.'

He twined the end of his rope around the horn of his saddle and swung himself on to his horse. He pricked the animal with his spurs and it cantered forward, back the way it had come. Stumbling, the Kid was jerked along with it.

With his outfit broken up, with Pete Farman and his crowd on the warpath, Jumbo Jordan knew that it was useless to think of returning to Come Lucky.

He headed back for the Indian cave settlement, dragging the Kid captive behind him. The Kid's big black trailed along in the rear. They caught up with Dutch Henry. He grinned when he saw the Kid.

'You sure make a mighty fine pack-mule,' he sneered. An expression of rage contorted his features. 'Bust my hands, would you, you swine?'

He manoeuvred his pinto alongside and struck at the Kid with his spurred foot. The spur raked the Kid's side, tearing his shirt, drawing blood. Only the tightening of his mouth suggested how much the blow hurt him.

'Make the coyote run,' Dutch suggested.

Jordan grinned at the suggestion. He spurred his horse forward into a canter where the trail ran downhill a short distance. The Kid started to run to try to keep up. He stumbled, sank to his knees, was dragged along on them, twisting over and over. The lariat bit cruelly into his thin body; the rough surface of the trail tore at his flesh and clothing. Sweat soaked his clothes to chafe the raw flesh. The flesh wounds he had sustained during the gun battle in Come Lucky began to ache and throb. One began to bleed again. Desperately he fought to hang on to his swimming senses. And that was the way things were with him as Jordan reined in suddenly at the sight of the stretched-out girl lying unconscious beside the trail.

11

The four of them spent that night in the open beside the mountain stream, Jordan cursing that his plans had gone astray, Dutch Henry bemoaning the fact of his crippled hands. Without the rope ladder it had been impossible to get up to the cave settlement, but a whistle from Jordan had brought the old Indian woman to the cave entrance.

Shouted conversation between Jordan and the Indian woman, fragments of which had drifted across the valley to where the Cougar Kid lay, dead-beat, in the shadow of the trees, had seen a sack lowered at the end of a rope. Jordan had ridden back with it; emptied it out . . . coffee, bacon and the utensils that went with them.

While the Kid lay hogtied and Dutch Henry sat looking at his broken hands, Jordan gathered sticks and got a fire going. Gail helped him. Presently there arose the sizzling aroma of a meal. Rough and ready as it was, it smelled mighty good to the Kid. It was a long time since he had last eaten. But Jordan was taking no chances and he refused to loosen the whang string around the Kid's wrists. He pushed a pannikin of bacon and a mug of steaming coffee across the ground towards him.

'You'll manage without your hands if you're really hungry.' he said.

Gail Bronson darted him an angry, contemptuous glance.

She held the mug for the Kid to drink from; fed him the bacon. She did it with a curiously hurt, tender look in her soft eyes. It was the first time she had seen the Kid since that morning outside the dry-goods store in Come Lucky, and all that she had felt then suddenly swamped back on her with renewed emphasis. Tenderly, she bathed his cuts and bruises with water from the stream; bound his wounded arm with a strip torn from his own shirt. And with each action she let her hands linger a little longer than was really necessary. There was something virile, aggressively masculine about the Cougar Kid, and Gail Bronson felt it with every fibre of her being. Something inside her cried out for him. But if the Kid had any inkling of how she was feeling, he gave no sign.

They made a strange, motley company around the fire that Jordan had built as darkness came to that lost valley in the heart of the Sierras. The leaping flames lit their faces and lit up a whole host of curiously mixed emotions along with them. There was Dutch Henry, nursing his mangled hands, hatred in every glance he directed at the Cougar Kid. The Kid himself, his hands bound, his clothing torn, his body bruised and battered, but a hard, implacable look in his eyes . . . eyes which tried not to meet those of Gail Bronson, which refused to meet what was written there.

Jordan checked the cord around the

Kid's wrists before the last tattered remnants of daylight finally faded over the purple hills, took his guns away from him, and used the lariat to fasten his legs. It was very cool in the valley once the sun had gone. Gail Bronson moved closer to the dying fire, shivering a little. But there was nothing anyone could do about that. The Kid, as Jumbo and Dutch Henry stretched themselves out for the night, rolled over on to his side and tested his bonds in the shadow of his body. But there was no future to it. Jordan had known what he was about. He thought of Gail Bronson and his eyes narrowed. But Jumbo had thought of that possibility, too. Before turning in he had fastened a length of whang to the girl's ankle, the other end to his own wrist. Undue movement on her part would bring him awake in an instant.

It was typical of the Kid that once having resigned himself to the fact that there was nothing he could do he should roll over and doze off. Typical, too, that he should sleep the deep, peaceful, dreamless sleep of a man who hasn't a care in the world.

The Cougar Kid hadn't. Confident — even arrogantly confident — of his own ability to find a way out of the mess he was in when the time came, he was content to let the morrow take care of itself.

But the first tinge of dawn over the hills found him instantly awake — eyes open, body motionless — poised, tense, the way a mountain cat is when it wakes.

Jumbo Jordan was awake at the first sign of dawn, too; up, striding about, unfastening the cord which linked him with Gail Bronson, kicking Dutch Henry into wakefulness. He seemed, somehow, a new man. The same Jumbo Jordan, yet different. Eyeing him, the Kid decided that Jumbo had made up his mind about something during the night.

He had. He had resigned himself to the inevitable. He knew that as far as

Come Lucky was concerned his race was run. And when a man's race is run, there is only one thing to do about it — pull out, head for new pastures. He had the girl, and, looking at her in that torn gingham frock, he decided that she was compensation enough for a whole lot of things. He had money salted away — in Dodge City, Abilene and across the Rio Grande in Mexico. He had made up his mind that that was where he would head — across the Rio Grande. And the girl would go with him. But before he went he had a score to settle with the ranchers of the Come Lucky territory.

He rolled a cigarette and thought of those eighteen thousand head of cattle rounded up ready for the long trek north. A stampede is easily started. Just get a few steers on the move and the rest will follow, panic communicating itself from animal to animal. And if the stampede should head them south into the wild, broken country flanking the Rio Grande . . . well, a man who knew what he was about might get a bunch of Mexes together and drive the steers that survived the stampede the rest of the way across the Border.

After they had eaten he took Dutch Henry aside. He didn't tell Dutch all that was in his mind, for Jordan was the type of man who did not believe in letting his left hand know what his right was doing.

'Look, Dutch,' he said, 'we've gotta get out of this. We'll get clear of the hills and you take the girl and head south. Follow the river-line. It will bring you straight down to the Border. Cross over and wait for me in Pedras Negras.'

Dutch shook his bearded face.

'I don't like it,' he said. 'The girl's gonna be troublesome. With a hornet's nest like this one about our ears, we'll have our work cut out to make the Border on our own. Wise up, Jumbo. Ditch the girl while there's still time.'

Jumbo said: 'The girl won't give any trouble. Not while you've got the Cougar Kid along.'

Dutch raised his bushy eyebrows.

Jumbo said, his voice trembling with jealous fury: 'She's gone on the guy. Surely you can see that. Anyone can see it. You've only got to watch the way she looks at him when she thinks no one's looking at her.'

It was true enough — even if the Kid didn't know; even if Gail Bronson was not yet prepared to admit it to herself. There was something about the Cougar Kid that she admired, pitied, loved and wanted. Something that had been there ever since that first night she had lashed him across the face — an action which had been as much a repression of her own inborn passions as it had been an action of real anger at her brother's condition. And now, seeing the Kid bound and bleeding, his lips set in a firm, thin line, his granite chip eyes hard and inscrutable, his spirit still unbroken, all that she felt had crystallised into a fierce, passionate longing for him.

Jumbo, with his own passionate

desires for the girl, knew how things were. Now he said: 'If she gives trouble, take it out of him. She won't give trouble a second time.'

Dutch said: 'I still don't like it.' He held up his crippled hands. 'Suppose he breaks loose.'

'He won't break loose,' said Jumbo, fiercely. 'He's hog-tied. All you've got to do is keep him hog-tied. You're not scared of him, are you?'

Dutch's eyes flickered apprehensively.

'Sure I'm scared of him. Hog-tied or not, he's a devil. I saw what he did back there in Come Lucky. There were six of us and only one of him. But he tore us apart. He fanned those damned guns of his — '

'Blast your hide,' Jumbo cut in on him. 'He hasn't got any guns now. You'll have his guns.'

'I can't use them.' Again Dutch held up his crippled hands.

'You'll use them all right if you've got to. That left forefinger can still squeeze a trigger. Here.'

He reached for the Kid's white-butted guns and thrust them into the empty holsters at Dutch's hips.

'Watch the girl. She'll set him free if she gets half a chance.'

Dutch nodded.

'I'll watch her.'

Inside him, he was thinking: 'Sure I'll watch her. For just as long as you're in gunshot. Then they both get it — the pair of them — and I'm high-tailing it for the Border on my lonesome. I'm not taking chances.'

They walked back to where the Kid and Gail Bronson sat together. She had made no attempt to set him free. She knew it was useless — at the moment. Without guns, he would have been shot down before he could even have got to his horse.

Jordan unlashed the Kid's ankles, kicked him to his feet. There was no need for the kicking, but the devil in him had to find some sort of an out. The Kid winced at the kick — and his wincing was echoed by the look of anguish in Gail Bronson's eyes.

Jordan saddled his own horse and Dutch's pinto. The Kid's big black was still saddled from the night before. It had refused to let Jordan come near it.

The lariat was fastened about the Kid's body again and the other end to the saddle-horn of Dutch's horse. Jordan looked at the Kid.

'Whether we treat the girl the same way is up to you, Cougar. She can ride that black of yours if you can persuade him to let her.'

The Kid whistled the black over. It came obediently. He stood with his face close to its muzzle. A flick of his head motioned the girl to mount.

As soon as her foot touched the stirrup the black edged away. The Kid made coaxing noises. The girl tried again. This time the black stood perfectly still. Jumbo Jordan took hold of the black's hitching rein and knotted it to his own reins.

'OK,' he said. 'Let's go.'

They set off, the Kid again stumbling

and slithering along in his high-heeled riding boots — a tortured, pathetic figure. But the agonies he was going through refused to show on his rawboned face. Whenever Gail Bronson looked back he gave her a flickering, ghost of a smile of encouragement.

The sun was hot in the heavens as they came down from the Sierras into the river valley. Jumbo motioned them to stop. He passed the black's hitching rein to Dutch Henry.

'This is where we part company,' he said. 'Don't forget — if the girl gives trouble, beat hell outa the Kid.' He looked back to where the Kid stood, swaying and unsteady, at the end of the lariat. 'And viceversa,' he added. Then he sent his horse plunging across the river and up the slope beyond.

The others turned south, the horses cantering along the loose shale that fringed the river. But quarter of a mile downstream Dutch reined in again and swung himself from the saddle.

'This is as far as we go,' he said.

'Jumbo said for me to take the pair of you over the Border, but me — I've got other ideas.'

His left hand fumbled for the Kid's white-butted gun slung at his thigh. He winced as his raw palm encountered it. Slowly, his twisted fingers drew it from its holster. Never again would Dutch Henry possess his old speed with a gun. Never again, perhaps, would his right hand be capable of pulling a gun at all.

The gun in his left hand shook a little as he brought it up. He had to reach over with his right to pull back the hammer. He stood about eight paces from the Kid, the gun levelled. He couldn't possibly miss at that range. 'You first,' he said, grimly.

A look of pain clouded his eyes as his crippled forefinger tightened about the trigger.

'No!' shrieked the girl. 'No!'

The rocky bluff which fringed the river threw back the echoes of her terrified shout.

The Kid's tongue came out and

licked dry, cracked lips. He measured the distance between himself and Dutch. He knew he could never make it.

The boom of the white-butted Colt echoed all the way along the rock face as Dutch fired.

12

Even as Dutch fired, Gail Bronson was urging the Kid's big black frantically towards him. The hitching rein, fastened to the pinto, prevented it going all the way. It swung round, its haunch striking Dutch, knocking him off balance. The shell hit a rock two feet ahead of the Kid and ricochetted away towards the river with a thin whine. Dutch went sprawling.

In an instant the Kid was leaping towards him. The lariat jerked him up short.

'Quick,' he shouted. 'Unfasten that lariat.'

Dutch was stumbling to his feet even as the girl's frantic fingers reached for the rope twisted round the pinto's saddlehorn. It came free just as Dutch stood up. The gun was still in his hand, but the Kid gave no thought to that.

Gun or not, he had to go for Dutch. It was either that or be shot down in cold blood.

His bent head, as he bounded forward, took the gunman full in the chest. This time the gun went sprawling as Dutch stumbled back. He made a dive for it, but the Kid was there first, kicking it out of reach. His hands might be lashed, but his feet were not. He lashed out again with his foot.

The blow took Dutch in the stomach. His right hand went for the other gun slung at his hip, but his crippled fingers were unable to grip it. He looked at the Kid and saw death in those yellow-flecked eyes. Desperately, he hit out with his left hand. The blow took the Kid full in the face, splitting his cracked lips. Again and again Dutch hit him, wincing himself with the agony of each blow he delivered.

Gail Bronson jumped down from the black and raced for the gun lying there among the loose shale. But before she could scoop it up the Kid's knee was again driving up hard into Dutch's stomach. His bound hands crashed up into the man's face, driving him back. Dutch slipped and went sprawling. Even as he fell the Kid's boot took him in the face. The Kid was beyond reason at that moment — just a mad, insensate, fighting machine — fighting, because he had to, with his feet instead of his hands, with his high-heeled riding boots instead of his guns.

Dutch screamed wildly as one of those high heels came smashing down on him. He rolled over and over in a frantic endeavour to get away. But always the Kid was there, like a wild horse, pounding, smashing, flailing. All the torment he had endured being dragged on foot behind a horse through the mountain crags of the Sierras, all the hate that had stored up inside him, found an out at that moment.

He kicked and went on kicking until he had pounded Dutch insensible; until insensibility had become death. The girl stood, gun in one hand, like a statue frozen in stone, not wanting to look yet unable to tear her eyes away from the cruel spectacle.

Her voice was hoarse croak as she said: 'He's dead.'

The Kid heard her even above the pounding of his own heart, his frantic breathing, the hate and fury that was like scalding steam in his brain.

He stopped, suddenly motionless except for the rise and fall of his chest.

'Yes,' he said presently, his voice completely without any sort of expression. 'He's dead.'

He held out his bound hands. The wrists were raw and bleeding where the rope had cut them.

'Get this off me,' he said.

The girl put down the gun and moved towards him. She still seemed dazed by the spectacle she had witnessed. Her fingers plucked at the knots. But the struggle had pulled them tight and it was a long time before the Kid was free. He stood rubbing his chafed wrists, his breathing still not quite normal.

Suddenly the girl reached up. Her hands took him by the shoulders and her lips were pressed hard against his.

The Kid looked at her with expressionless eyes as she let go of him and backed away as though half-ashamed at betraying the emotions within her.

He smiled. 'Well, what do you know,' he said.

He collected his guns and thrust them into their holsters, unhitched the black from the pinto and swung himself into the saddle.

'Think you can ride that thing?' he said.

The girl said: 'It's a horse, isn't it?'

The Kid shook his head.

'No,' he said. 'It's a pinto. Dutch may have been a gunslinger, but he was no cowhand. No cow-hand would ever pick himself a pinto. They scare too easy.'

'How about you?' asked Gail. 'Aren't you a cowhand?'

A strange mingled look of anger and regret clouded the Kid's deepset eyes.

'It don't matter what I am,' he said. And that was all anyone could ever get out of him whenever the question of his past came up.

'Hurry it up,' he said. 'There's work to do.'

The girl paused in the act of swinging herself on to the pinto.

'What do you mean — work to do?' she asked, almost as though she knew the answer and was a little afraid of it.

The Kid said quietly: 'I've still got a score to settle with Jumbo Jordan.'

She followed him on the pinto as he pricked the black into a canter.

'But you don't know where he is,' she said.

The Kid looked at her with eyes that were like frozen pools.

'It don't matter where he is,' he said. 'I'll find him.'

*   *   *

A mile away another party of horsemen pricked their mounts into a canter at

171

almost the same instant. Pete Farman and his crowd, after being outsmarted by the Kid, had continued searching the foothills till sundown. They had camped out; been up at day-break; gone on with the search. Now, as the echoes of Dutch's shot reached them on the warm, sunbaked air, they sat their horses, motionless an instant, while they pinpointed the direction of the sound. Then they were off, riding as hard as the uneven nature of the ground permitted, converging in the direction from which the shot had come.

It was Pete Farman who first saw the two riders following the line of the river valley.

'Got them, by jingo.'

He unshipped his rifle, brought it quickly to his shoulder, squeezed the trigger. The shell struck an outcrop of rock maybe two yards ahead of the Cougar Kid's horse, ricochetting off. In a flash the Kid was out of the saddle, crouched down behind the horse, peering under its belly in the direction from which the shot had come. His guns were in his hands. One of them waved in Gail's direction — a gesture for her to take cover.

High above them, a fair way off, Pete Farman yelled to those with him.

'Spread out, fellers, and close in on 'em.'

His rifle cracked again in the direction of the running figure which was Gail Bronson. It was Matt Bronson who grabbed at it and jerked the barrel to one side even as Farman fired.

'Hold it, Pete — that's my sister.'

Pete Farman lowered his rifle.

They spurred their horses along a narrow trail of sorts running downhill between two mighty crags. It brought them out no more than a long spit from the river.

Matt Bronson made his hands into a loud-hailer; yelled through them.

'Gail, this is me — Matt. Who's that with you?' Cautiously the girl straightened up behind the rock to which she had scurried for safety.

The Kid said: 'Stay where you are, Miss Bronson. Tell the feller to show himself.'

She called out: 'Where are you, Matt?'

'Here, Sis.' He rode out from behind the crag. Behind him Pete Farman raised his rifle to give him cover. Bronson said again: 'Who's that with you?'

The girl sprang from behind the rock and raced towards him.

'It's the Kid — the Cougar Kid.'

Pete Farman said: 'Tell him to throw down his guns and come out with his hands up.'

The Kid answered for himself.

'Nothing doing.'

The girl stopped short.

'You don't understand,' she said. 'The Kid doesn't have to give up his guns. He saved me.'

Farman said, uncompromisingly: 'He's one of Jumbo Jordan's men.'

They might have got things straightened out but for another of the Pete

Farman crowd. He had spread out with the others when Pete gave the word, worked his way round, begun to close in. He slid from his saddle and went forward on foot, worming his way among the rocks which fringed the river. From where he was he could not see Farman and Matt Bronson. But he had a nice clear view of the Cougar Kid crouching beneath the belly of the black. He brought up his rifle and took a snapshot. The bullet whined past the Kid's ear like an angry mosquito. He swung round, working the hammers of the white-butted Colts. The distance was too far for accurate work with a Colt, but it had the effect of driving the man to cover.

Matt Bronson slid from his saddle as his sister raced towards him.

'Tell 'em to stop, Matt,' she cried, flinging herself into his arms.

But it was too late for that. The rest of the Farman crowd, scattered among the rocks, were using their rifles now. The Kid, driven to ground by their fire, did the only thing he could do. He whistled up the black to its feet, swung himself into the saddle and raced for the river. Once in midstream he slid from the saddle again and swam alongside the black so that only his head showed. Bullets made miniature fountains around him as he swam.

Gail Bronson sobbed in her brother's arms. 'He saved my life. He saved my life,' she repeated over and over again. 'Don't let them kill him. Stop them.'

Pete Farman did his best, but those with him were too scattered to heed his words. Already three more horses were cresting the river in pursuit of the Kid.

The Kid, looking back, saw them and grinned to himself. Yesterday they had chased him into the hills; now they were chasing him out of them. Not that it mattered a whole heap. He was going the way Jumbo Jordan had gone — and he had a score to settle with Jordan.

On the far side of the river Gail Bronson raced for the pinto.

'We've got to catch them,' she cried.

176

'They mustn't kill him. He saved my life.'

She would have urged the pinto into the river had not Pete Farman caught at the rein. 'I'll go after them,' he said. 'You and Matt ride upstream aways. There's a ford there.'

He left them to explain to the rest of the party as they came riding up. He plunged his mount into the river and clattered up the incline the far side. Ahead stretched the vast flatness of the range. The Kid and the three riders pursuing him were already no more than dustclouds in the distance. Farman, as he urged his horse into a gallop, doubted his mount's ability to overtake them.

13

Jumbo Jordan reined in his horse, wetted a thick forefinger and held it up to test the wind. He grinned to himself. It could hardly have been better had he ordered it specially.

He had ridden in a wide semi-circle to avoid Come Lucky and was now several miles north of that sun-bleached, ugly little township. Due north, too, of the great milling herd being got together for the long trek up the Chisholm Trail to Dodge City. The bulk of the herd was about a mile south, where the work of branding and tallying still went on, but many of the animals had strayed far afield. No one worried about that. You cannot keep a herd of eighteen thousand animals in one tight compact bunch. The outriders, on their endless circuits, were continually chivvying back small groups

of animals which had strayed too far.
There was one such group now where
Jumbo Jordan sat his horse. Maybe two
hundred beef steers. Maybe more.

He slipped from the saddle, gathered
together some scattered brushwood and
lighted a small fire. He lighted it where
the coarse, dry grass was thickest. He
watched little ripples of blue and yellow
flame begin to flicker among the grass
itself.

He flung himself into the saddle,
rode on about fifty yards, lighted
another fire. Then another . . . and
another . . . until he had half-a-dozen of
them burning in a wide semi-circle,
with the flames of each flickering out
along the dried grass towards one
another.

The nearest steer raised its head and
sniffed the breeze. It went on cropping.
Another raised its head, stirring uneasily. The half-dozen fires became a
continuous chain of flame nearly three
hundred yards long. It began to crackle,
to leap forward under a pall of

low-hanging smoke.

First one steer, then another, shied away, began to trot. The crackle of the fire became a roar. The smoke became a dense, low-hanging cloud. The trot of the frightened animals became a canter. The canter became a gallop as wind fanned the flames towards them.

Jordan rode clear of the smoke on to a ridge of higher land where he could watch.

A mile away, where the branding operations were in progress, a cowhand lifted his head, nose twitching. His eyes widened. He lifted a hand and pointed.

'Fire!'

In an instant the branding and tallying were forgotten. Orders were shouted. Men raced for their saddles, grabbing up empty sacks as they went. Others spurred furiously towards the main herd.

There is nothing upsets a herd of cattle so much as fire. A tongue of flame will turn steers from meek, submissive creatures into raging tornadoes, threshing this way and that, smashing down everything that stands in their way in a mad panic.

And that is perhaps the only thing your average cowhand really fears — a stampede. A big herd on the rampage, heads down, horns swinging, hoofs thundering, their hocks rattling against one another like pool-balls in a bag.

They heard it now as they swung out on their horses to quieten the main herd — that distant rattle of hocks. Saw ahead of the cloud of smoke which was the fire another cloud — the dustcloud kicked up by the hoofs of the frightened beasts.

'Head 'em off,' came a yell. 'Don't let 'em connect with the main herd.'

But it was too late. A long way too late. Already that vast brown sea of cattle was becoming restless; horns tossing white like foam-crested rollers in the tumbling surf. They could smell the distant smoke; hear the thunder of hoofs.

Cowhands spurred out to meet the approaching stampede; tried to turn it;

to get it running round in circles until its momentum should die away. It was no good. The stampeding beasts over-ran them; linked up with the main herd.

Sometimes it needs only one terrified steer to start a stampede. And there were two to three hundred of them in a bunch that came galloping south in terror of the fires Jumbo Jordan had started. They plunged headlong into the main herd, already restless and uneasy.

In a flash, it seemed, that whole vast brown sea of cattle was on the move, hoofs thundering up a giant dustcloud which blotted out the sun. The whole vast range became a grey and acrid place swamped with a thunder of hoofs which drowned the sound of hoarse, urgent shouts and the boom of Colts as men swerved and darted on nimble cow-ponies in an endeavour to stem the tide of death and destruction.

Cowhands, caught in that first great rush as the whole herd broke into motion, were bowled over, swamped, trampled beneath those threshing hoofs. Others swung aside in time, urging their ponies through the outer fringes of the great herd to safety . . . to sit their saddles, grey-faced, and watch that tide of death sweep forward. Steers themselves went down to die under the hoofs of the others. Nothing, once it lost its footing, could live in that sea of destruction. Onwards it swept — relentless, inexorable, terrifying. And three miles ahead, right in the path of the stampede, lay Come Lucky.

And between the two — the herd and the town — rode the Cougar Kid.

He saw what was happening even as he rode — saw the stampeding cattle spread out in a great line which seemed to blot out the whole horizon. He was galloping parallel with the front of the stampede when the distant ominous rumble of it first reached him. In a flash all thoughts of the pursuing horsemen, of Jumbo Jordan, were forgotten.

He turned his horse and headed hell-for-leather for Come Lucky. Behind him came Death . . . Death in the shape of the thundering hoofs of eighteen thousand stampeding steers. But it wasn't that that made the Kid ride the big rawboned black flat out. It was the thought of the folk in Come Lucky. Rough, tough they might be. Cowhands, good-time girls, gamblers, drifters, flotsam and jetsam of all sorts, drawn together by the lure of easy money and the call of the great open spaces. There were men among them who would be hanged on sight if they went back where they had come from. But they were human for all that. Flesh and blood. They had to be warned.

The Kid raked the black's flanks with his spurs, lashing it into a rawboned bunch of lather. Sweat streamed down his own face and dust caked his lips.

He rode into Come Lucky's solitary main street — a sweat-ridden, dust-covered, yelling, ghost of a man.

'Out. Everybody out. The herd's on the rampage and heading this way.'

It brought them to doors and windows with questioning mouths and urgent eyes.

'Listen,' said someone.

They listened, breathless, waiting. It was like distant drums.

Silence became bedlam. Order became panic. Horses were saddled up; belongings tossed frantically from windows; a buggy went clattering out of the street. But there were many who stood and wrung their hands. An elderly woman caught at the Kid's sleeve.

'What'll I do, mister? I ain't got no horse.'

The girls from the Golden Nugget were fighting for places aboard a buckboard. Already it held more than it could safely carry.

The Kid looked at it all with hard, weary eyes.

There was only one thing to do. He spurred his big black over to the store, sprang from the saddle, raced inside. He grabbed a drum of kerosene, punched it wide open with a pick. The whole length of the sidewalk he raced, pouring oil as he went. It was empty by the time he got to the Nugget. He pitched the drum in through the swing-doors; fumbled in his pocket for a match.

Lew Reardon charged towards him.

'You ain't firing my place,' he said.

The Kid's tired eyes looked at him.

'It's the only way, Reardon. Fire's the only thing that will stop them. We've got to fire the whole of this side of the street. With luck, we can stop the flames spreading across.'

'Not my place, Cougar.'

'Sorry, Reardon.'

A match flared in the Kid's hands. Reardon's own hands went for the guns slung at his hips. The match dropped. There was a tiny explosive pouf. The kerosene-soaked sidewalk became a wall of flame. It flared between the Kid and Reardon, forcing them both back, separating them from each other.

The dry, sun-bleached timbers of Come Lucky crackled and burned. Flames spread along the wooden sidewalk, along the hitching rails, climbed the supporting poles, licked at the walls and sloping roofs. On the other side of the street, folk soaked the crazy, wood-built structures with what little water there was. Men climbed on to roofs to trample out the flying sparks. One side of the street was now nothing more than one vast sheet of flame. And through the flames, guns in hand, came Lew Reardon.

'Blast your hide, Cougar. All my takings for the past three months were in there.'

There was a crazy look in Reardon's eyes — the look of greed when it sees riches vanishing before its eyes.

'Go for your guns, Cougar.'

The Kid was fast, but not that fast. He knew he would never get his guns out in the time; never be given the chance. Reardon's guns were already in his hands, trigger-fingers trembling. He would be blasting even as the Kid's fingers touched those white-butted Colts.

Help came from an unexpected quarter — the wild, piercing shriek of a woman in agony. Through the smoke and flames they saw her at one of the windows of the Golden Nugget. It was Lila, the Mexican girl. Her face was screwed up with pain.

'My ankle eet ees trapped.'

Turning, the Kid forgotten, Reardon charged towards the flames.

The Kid yelled hoarsely. 'Come back, you fool. It's no good. You haven't a chance . . .'

Then he was racing after Reardon. The flames swallowed both of them.

The door of the Nugget was a ring of flame. The Kid went through it. Flames plucked at his clothing; danced on his flesh. He beat them out with frantic hands. Smoke filled his throat; started him choking. He drew his neckerchief up about his mouth, bent his head, raced for the door of the office. A burning beam crashed ahead of him. He jumped over it; ran on.

Smoke swirled in the tiny room which Reardon had used as an office. The girl was beside the window. A tall cupboard had overturned pinning her foot. Reardon was struggling to push the cupboard clear. Flames danced round his hands as he worked.

With a mighty heave Reardon got the cupboard clear. The girl sank unconscious to the floor. And even as Reardon moved towards her the smoke got him, too. He sank down on his knees, coughing, gasping, racking his innards.

The Kid bent over him.

Bloodshot eyes looked up at him. Reardon shook his head.

'The girl. Get the girl out,' he said, gasping.

The Kid let go of him and dashed for the girl. He hoisted her into his arms. The window was too small. He raced back the way he had come. It was like going through an inferno. His senses reeled, but he charged on. Something hit him across the shoulder, sent him staggering. He fetched up against the burning bar, regained his balance, staggered for the doorway. It was a solid sheet of flame now. He hit it on the run; burst through. Then he was sprawling full-length in the dusty roadway, gasping for breath.

Willing hands helped him to his feet. Reardon! He was still in there. The Kid made a move back towards the sheet of flame which was all there was of that side of Come Lucky. Rough hands grabbed him back. He tried to fight them off, but he was too far gone.

'Reardon,' he gasped. 'He's still in there.'

Someone said: 'Damned good riddance to bad rubbish, if you ask me. He should have known better than to go back for his dough.'

Only the Cougar Kid knew that that epitaph to Lew Reardon was not deserved. His last actions had been courageous.

A shout sent the whole crowd of them racing along the street.

'It's halted the herd.'

It had, indeed. The foremost steers were already swinging away from the burning township in a vast arc, their speed diminishing.

The Kid whistled for his big black.

'Let's get out there,' he yelled. 'We can get 'em moving in a circle now if we work at it.'

14

They did work. The rest of the day and far into the night. Tirelessly, unceasingly — cowhands, ranchers, every guy who could fork a horse. Heading the herd, turning it, heading it again. Letting it run itself to a standstill. They lost some, of course — little bunches of cattle that charged off into the blue. Scores of others died under the trampling hoofs of their fellows. But as the first star came out in the night sky the herd was stationary again. Uneasy, trembling, but stationary. It was only then that they had time to wonder how the stampede had started.

They found the remains of the brushwood fire Jumbo Jordan had started. Pete Farman and Matt Bronson were there — Gail Bronson was being looked after by Pete's mother at the Double Diamond — and they stood looking at the little piles of grey-white ash with lack-lustre eyes.

Farman said: 'That weren't no accident. Someone did that deliberately.'

Their eyes met. Matt Bronson said: 'There's only one man would do a thing like that.'

Farman nodded.

The Cougar Kid didn't say anything. He believed in actions — not words. Already he was swinging himself back into the saddle, of his big, rawboned black.

There was a low murmur from the rest of the crowd as they gazed at the remains of the brushwood fire. Farman said:

'Well, what are we waiting for? Know where I'd head if I'd done a trick like that?'

Heads nodded. They knew all right. The Border — Mexico — the Rio Grande. It was obvious.

Farman said: 'OK. Fan out then. He can't have got far. He'd be trapped this side of the herd till the stampede was under control. We'll comb every square mile between here and the Border.'

Luck was with them. They picked up Jumbo Jordan's trail fifteen miles from the Rio Grande — a drifting cowpoke had seen a big guy around twenty stone riding a horse the sort the Cougar Kid described.

'Passed him a mile or so back,' he said. 'His horse seemed to have gone lame on him.'

It had . . . and this is where I come into the picture.

I was a nipper of fourteen at the time. My old man was one of the homesteaders the ranchers used to curse about. Homesteaders and ranchers didn't get along so sweet. There was a reason for that. The homesteaders wanted to fence off the range to protect their crops; the ranchers wanted wide open spaces for their cattle to graze on. Sometimes it came to shooting between the two factions.

The old man and I were just outside

the barn, struggling to fix a busted plough, and Ma had just come across with the mid-morning coffee, when Jumbo Jordan rode into the yard, his horse limping a little. I didn't like the look of him — and I don't think the old man did either. His unshaven face was caked with alkali dust and his shirt was sticking to his big body with sweat. His eyes were strained and bloodshot. But the old man held the coffee-pot out to him.

'You sure look like you could do with a drink, stranger.'

Jumbo said, as he swung himself from the saddle: 'I could do with another horse. This one's gone lame on me.'

Pa shook his head.

'Sorry. Guess we've only got one horse and I ain't fixing to trade it.'

Jumbo's bloodshot eyes narrowed.

'Who said anything about trading?' The next minute his hand was nursing a gun. 'Where is it?'

Pa passed his tongue over his lips.

There was an obstinate look in his pale blue eyes; a tightening of the muscles around the jaw. But that moment the horse whinnied from inside the barn.

Jumbo gestured with the gun.

'Go get it,' he said. Pa hesitated. His own gun was back in the shack. Jumbo's big hand flashed out and grabbed me by the collar. He jerked me to him. I wriggled, but he held me tight.

'Go get it,' he said again. His Colt jabbed into my ribs. 'And no tricks, mind, or the kid gets his.'

'Don't you do it, Pa,' I yelled. It was a fool thing to do, but, like I said, I was only a nipper at the time.

Ma and the old man looked at each other apprehensively. Ma jerked her shawl tighter about her shoulders — something she always did when she was upset.

'Better do what the man says, Abe.'

The old man hesitated a moment longer, then walked away into the shadows of the barn. We heard the sounds as he saddled up. It was then that I saw the distant dust-cloud flying towards us across the range.

'Look,' I yelled, pointing.

I felt Jumbo's grasp tighten on my collar. He hustled me ahead of him towards the barn.

'Hurry it up, old man,' he said, menacingly.

There was a scurry of running feet. Jumbo whirled, taking me with him. It was Ma. What she had in mind no one will ever know. Maybe she was out to get Pop's gun from inside the shack. She was flying across the yard towards the shack, her shawl trailing in the wind behind her.

Jumbo yelled to her to stay where she was. Maybe she heard him; maybe not. But she went on running. I felt his gun taken away from my ribs.

'No,' I yelled. 'No.'

Another frantic wriggle had me free — but my own impetus sent me sprawling in the dust.

The Colt in Jumbo's hand boomed.

I saw Ma stop suddenly as though

she had fetched up against an invisible wall. She stayed that way for a moment. Then she half-twisted so that we could just see her face and slid in a heap.

The boom of the Colt brought the old man on the run from inside the barn. Scrambling to my feet, I saw the way his face was working as he flew at Jumbo.

'Why, you dirty, rotten — '

Words became meaningless sounds as one hand closed on Jumbo's wrist and the other pounded furiously at that fat, sweatbeaded, unshaven face. Jumbo was trying to bring his gunhand round in a position to fire; the old man was trying to stop him. I could see the veins standing out on the old man's forehead as he struggled. But slowly, surely, the gun came round. The spectacle held me petrified. I was rooted to the spot, wide-eyed, gaping. Even the fact that the approaching dustcloud had resolved itself into a man riding a big black as though his very life depended upon it could not break the spell for me.

The boom of Jumbo's Colt broke it though. He had got the gun round, pointing up, at close quarters. It blew half the old man's face away.

I bit my lip and tore across the yard. Jumbo must have whirled and fired. I heard the thud of the shell hitting the woodwork even as my trembling fingers grabbed the latch of the door. I threw it open as Jumbo's big feet pounded across the yard after me.

The old man's gun should have been on the dresser. It wasn't. There was no time to look for it. Jumbo was just outside the door now. I looked at the window and knew that I should never make it. I looked up at the big beams supporting the roof. My hands went up, closed over them and I drew myself up even as Jumbo stood framed in the doorway.

I lay very still, trying hard not to breathe. From where I was I could see him. He had only to look up to see me.

But he didn't look up. For at that moment a shell whammed through the window and buried itself into the rough timbers. A voice said:

'Com'n out, Jumbo. I know you're in there.'

Jumbo slammed the door shut and stood against it, his eyes roving the shack. He dropped on all fours, scuttling across the room to come up underneath the window. He squatted there, gun in hand.

'Come and get me,' he yelled.

'Sure will.'

There was silence for a time after that. Then a slithering sound from outside as though someone's clothes were rubbing against the timbers of the shack. Then a creaking sound from the next room as though someone had climbed in through the window and on to the bed. It was a very small sound, very remote, but I heard it. Jumbo heard it, too, judging by the expression that crossed his face. Quietly, cautiously, he moved round until the table was between him and the next room. He crouched behind it, his gun barrel resting on the table edge. He was right beneath me. I saw his thumb take back the hammer as the door to the next room trembled a little and began to open.

I threw myself on to him just as he fired.

I hit him full between the shoulders, throwing him forward, smashing his face against the edge of the table, jerking his gunhand up so that the shell ploughed harmlessly into the beam on which I had been lying. I didn't plan it that way. It just happened.

Cursing, he threw me to one side as he straightened himself up. I was looking straight down the barrel of his Colt as I rolled over on the dirt floor.

But he never fired. Someone else fired ahead of him — from the direction of the door leading into the next room — and Jumbo was nursing fingers that dripped blood while I went scuttling across the room to retrieve the Colt which had been blown from his hand.

'Guess you saved my life, kid,' said a voice from the doorway.

Maybe I did save the Cougar Kid's

life that day; maybe I didn't. He always said I did, but when I came to know him better — came to realize his devilish quickness with a gun — I also came to doubt whether he needed the help of a fourteen-year-old kid to get the better of Jumbo Jordan in gunplay.

I picked up Jumbo's big Colt and forced back the hammer with my other hand.

'Steady on there,' said the Cougar Kid. 'Those things go bang.'

I gritted my teeth. 'I know,' I said. 'You don't have to tell me. I've handled them before.'

I pointed the gun at Jumbo Jordan. 'He's my meat,' I said. 'He killed my ma and pa.'

The Cougar Kid looked at me; looked at Jumbo; said:

'I guess the boy's got something there, Jumbo.'

Jumbo may have been an out-and-out rogue, but he proved himself no coward.

'Blast yer hide, Cougar,' he snarled.

That moment there was a fresh clatter of hoofs in the yard outside and suddenly the shack was full of men.

The Cougar Kid said: 'You a mite late, Farman.'

Farman said: 'That black of yours may look ugly, but it's sure got some staying power.' He looked at me. 'Who's this?'

The Cougar Kid told him.

Farman said: 'You mean to say you were gonna let the kid kill Jumbo?'

The Cougar Kid's eyes were granite pinpoints.

'Sure. Why not? Jumbo killed his folks.'

Someone else said: 'Any killing ought to be done nice and legal. How can we hope to have law and order in this territory if we don't start imposing some ourselves. We've got to give the guy a fair trial.'

The idea caught on. Others nodded assent. The Cougar Kid grinned at me.

'You can put that gun away, son. You ain't gonna do no killing.'

They hogtied Jumbo Jordan's hands,

took him outside, mounted him on Pa's horse and tied his feet under the belly. The rest of them swung themselves into the saddle. I stood looking at them, Jumbo's gun stuck into the bellyband of my cut-down pants.

Farman said: 'What about the kid?'

The one whose name was Matt Bronson said: 'He can't stay on here now his folks are dead. Guess he could come and live with Sis and me when we get the Crazy Y re-built.'

The Cougar laughed — one of the few times anyone really heard him laugh.

'Oh, no, you don't,' he said. 'He saved my life. That makes him my sidekick.'

He reached over and swung me up into the saddle in front of him. I felt real fine and dandy sitting up there with a two-gun man like the Cougar Kid.

'We're gonna be pardners, ain't we, son?' he said.

'Sure,' I said. The way I said it, it didn't mean anything. But the way things turned out, we were partners for close on twenty years.

15

They convened a court of justice that night in the big main room of the Double Diamond ranch-house. The long, scarred table was pushed against one wall and twelve of them sat on it, their long legs dangling. They were the jury. They elected the Cougar Kid as judge and he sat on a barrel at the far end of the room. Pete Farman somehow elected himself to the double role of official prosecutor and foreman of the jury. Yes, the whole proceedings were as crude as that, but no one there saw anything ludicrous in the situation. It was range justice — rough and ready, but seldom wrong.

The big flickering kerosene lamps cast a ghastly yellow glare over the proceedings. The leaping firelight threw grotesque shadows on the adobe walls. Jumbo Jordan, his piglike eyes very bloodshot, one hand bandaged sat in a high-backed chair facing the jury. His eyes flickered apprehensively from face to face. He saw no mercy in those range-wise eyes and knew that his race was run. He started to his feet.

'If you're gonna kill me, then for Pete's sake get it over and done with. This is a farce. You know what the verdict is gonna be as well as I do.'

The Cougar Kid said, cynically: 'The prisoner will kindly resume his seat.'

There was a chuckle at that — an unpleasant, threatening chuckle.

They pushed Jumbo back into his chair.

'Siddown you,' said Zeke Martin, fierce as a mountain lion now that Jumbo's race was so obviously run. 'You're gonna be tried fair and square whether you like it or not.'

They crowded into the room, all those who had suffered at the hands of Jumbo Jordan in the past. They leaned, with gangling legs, thumbs hooked in gunbelts, against the walls or sat crosslegged on the bare boards of the floor.

Peter Farman strode up and down the room.

'Guess I don't need to tell you why we're here.' A menacing murmur told him he was dead right there, but he went on talking. 'The prisoner — Jumbo Jordan — is accused of a whole heap of things, but I guess one or two of them will do to be going on with. We'll start with the kidnapping of Miss Bronson. You all know pretty well what happened.' He looked round the grim, weatherbeaten faces. 'Jordan here set fire to the Crazy Y and kidnapped Miss Bronson — '

Jordan licked his thick lips; leaned forward a little in his chair. He said:

'What you're a-saying ain't evidence, Farman. You should have Miss Bronson here to say I kidnapped her.'

What he hoped to gain by it no one will ever know. The whole crowd of them could have talked from then till doomsday and it wouldn't have made any difference to the final verdict. That was a foregone conclusion. But a man will try almost any wriggle he can think of when he sees death closing in on him.

Pete Farman stopped his pacing and looked at the Cougar Kid.

The Kid nodded.

'He's right,' he said. 'Miss Bronson's gotta say it for herself.'

Zeke Martin muttered: 'What does it matter who says what? The guy's as guilty as hell. We all know it.'

The Cougar Kid looked at him through narrowed eyes.

'I understood as how I was elected judge of this hyar court.' He paused, one hand on the butt of his gun. He looked round, but no one said anything. 'That being so, what I says goes. And I say that Jordan's right. He's entitled to have Miss Bronson say what she's gotta say for herself.'

Hope flickered in Jordan's eyes, only to die again as Farman said: 'Well, that's easy done.' He swung round on

Matt Bronson. 'Go fetch your sister down, Matt.'

Gail came down in an old-fashioned, high-necked frock Pete's mother had loaned her. Her eyes flickered apprehensively around the room; brightened when they saw the Cougar Kid. There was no answering brightness in the Kid's eyes. This was his revenge over the man who had fooled him and he wasn't going to forego an instant of it. He was like that — implacable, unforgiving, bitter.

He said: 'Give Miss Bronson a chair.'

They fetched her one. Pete Farman said:

'Gail, we want you to tell us what happened the night Jordan kidnapped you. Take your time now.'

The Cougar Kid said, tersely: 'It ain't been proved that anyone kidnapped anyone yet.'

Hesitatingly, her eyes flickering restlessly, Gail Bronson told of what had happened. Of how Comanche Bill Tucson had set fire to the window drapes of the Crazy Y.

Jumbo pounded the arms of his high-backed chair.

'Did you hear me tell him to fire them?' he demanded.

Gail licked her lips. 'Well — no — not exactly.'

Jumbo glared round him.

'See,' he said. 'It was Comanche — not me. I got Miss Bronson outa there when he did it.'

It wasn't true, of course. Not by a long chalk. And Gail Bronson had only to tell about the cave in the Sierras to tear Jumbo's whole story to bits. She moistened her lips. Womanlike, she felt suddenly sorry for Jordan. She said, unaccountably: 'Oh, let him go. What's happened is over and done with. I'm safe — that's all that matters. He's learned his lesson.'

Her brother said, angrily: 'Like hell he has. What about the Crazy Y? It's gonna take all this year's profits to re-build the place.'

Pete Farman dug his hands in his

pockets; rocked himself back on his heels. 'And that ain't all,' he said. 'What about the stampede? What about the guys who died in that?'

Jordan's beefy face was very white. He was fighting a battle in which the verdict had already gone against him — but he went on fighting.

'You can't prove I started the stampede,' he mumbled.

'OK,' said Pete. He pointed at me. 'Well, what about the kid's folks? You killed them. The kid saw you.'

Jumbo licked his thick lips.

'Who's gonna take a kid's word?' he said.

Someone said: 'Let the boy tell us.'

It became a chorus: 'Yeah — let the boy tell us.'

The Cougar Kid pounded with the flat of his hand for silence. 'Hold it,' he said. 'This is a court of law — not the Golden Nugget.'

That got a laugh — a laugh that had little humour in it.

Someone pushed me forward.

Pete Farman put his hand on my shoulder. 'Tell us what happened, son.'

I told them — in nervous, broken sentences. There was dead silence while I spoke and you could hear the spit of the logs in the hearth as the flames ate at them. When I was through there was still silence . . . the silence of hard, grim faces looking at Jumbo Jordan as his tongue licked nervous lips. Only Gail Bronson wasn't looking at him. Her face was hidden in her hands.

Zeke Martin broke the silence, starting forward, hand on gun.

'What the hell do we keep haggling about?' he demanded. 'We know the feller's guilty. Let's say so and get it over.'

Pete Farman looked across at the jury seated on the big table by the far wall.

'What do you say, boys?'

The end man nodded his head. 'Sure he's guilty.' Farman's eyes travelled along the line. 'Guilty.' 'Sure guilty as hell.' 'String the coyote up.'

Nods.

Farman looked at the Cougar Kid.

'Well, do we, Kid? Guess you're the judge, having been elected sich.'

The Kid got down off his barrel and walked towards Jordan, one hand scratching the back of the other. His face was quite expressionless; his eyes imponderable. He said:

'This hyar court finds you guilty, Jordan — guilty of kidnapping, arson, murder and pretty well every shot in the book I guess. I hereby sentence you to be taken outa here and strung up from the nearest tree,' then, as an afterthought, 'God rest your soul.'

Not quite the words a real judge would have used maybe, but their meaning was the same, and their effect more terrifying to the condemned man.

Jumbo rose hesitatingly to his feet.

'Look,' he said. 'I've got a stack of money cached away. Enough to re-build the Crazy Y a dozen times over. I'll hand it over if you let me go.'

'No,' I yelled. I grabbed at Jumbo's

arm. 'Money won't bring my ma and pa back.'

The Cougar Kid put his arm around my shoulder. He looked at me, then at Jumbo again. He shook his head.

'No dice, Jumbo.' He smiled. 'You're gonna swing, friend.'

'Like hell I am.'

Jumbo still had one card to play — and he played it. Pete Farman was nearest him. Before anyone could do anything about it Jumbo's bandaged hand had plucked Farman's gun from its holster. It was the last forlorn, desperate throw of a broken man. Jumbo had nothing to lose. He held the gun pointed straight at Gail Bronson. She was only four feet from him. He couldn't possibly have missed at that range.

'Go on,' he gritted. 'Blast me. You'll get me all right — you can't miss — but I'll get her.'

The Cougar Kid said, lazily: 'Not with Farman's gun you won't. It ain't loaded.'

It was. But Jumbo did what the Kid wanted him to do. He looked down at the gun in his hand. In that split-second of time the Kid acted.

Even those closest to him never saw him draw. There was just a fleeting vision of blurred hands; the crash of gunfire. Jumbo staggered back as though he had been punched in the chest, Farman's gun falling from his hand, blood staining his shirt in three separate places. He was a dying man who was not yet dead.

But the Cougar Kid was out for revenge.

He said: 'You gonna die legal, Jordan, as a lesson to others.'

Jumbo was spitting blood as they mounted him on my pa's horse. He swayed like a drunken man as the crowd of them set off, with me riding up in front of the Cougar Kid. Maybe it was a trick of the moonlight, but it seemed to me that his eyes were already glazing when we reached the cotton-woods. Pa's old pony stood motionless beneath the trees as they dropped the noose around Jordan's neck and flung it over a branch. They didn't even bother to tie his wrists.

The Cougar Kid said to me: 'This pony of yours, son — does it come when you whistle it?'

'Sure does,' I said.

He nodded. He looked at Jordan.

'S'long, Jumbo,' he said. 'Knowing you wasn't so nice.'

Jumbo's eyes flickered and I saw that he wasn't dead. His mouth opened and he tried to say something, but only blood came out. The Kid gestured with his head. The crowd of us rode about twenty yards off. From there Jumbo was silhouetted against the moonlight which streamed through the trees.

The Cougar Kid said: 'He killed your pa and ma, son. Go ahead — hang him.'

I looked up at him. 'How?' I said.

He didn't really grin. His face just contorted a little. 'Whistle up that pony of yours,' he said.

My lips felt very dry as I pursed them up. I hadn't helped kill a man before. Then I thought of my ma and pa, lying there in the dust of the yard.

I whistled.

Obediently, the pony trotted towards me.

Jumbo Jordan came with it for the first few feet. Then the rope tightened about his neck; jerked him from the saddle. As the Cougar Kid lifted me from in front of him into the saddle of Pa's horse, Jumbo was still swinging a little at the end of the rope, toes hanging down, his head on one side, his eyes bulging horribly in the moonlight.

THE END

We do hope that you have enjoyed reading this large print book.

Did you know that all of our titles are available for purchase?

We publish a wide range of high quality large print books including:
Romances, Mysteries, Classics
General Fiction
Non Fiction and Westerns

Special interest titles available in large print are:
The Little Oxford Dictionary
Music Book, Song Book
Hymn Book, Service Book

Also available from us courtesy of Oxford University Press:
Young Readers' Dictionary
(large print edition)
Young Readers' Thesaurus
(large print edition)

For further information or a free brochure, please contact us at:
Ulverscroft Large Print Books Ltd.,
The Green, Bradgate Road, Anstey,
Leicester, LE7 7FU, England.
Tel: (00 44) **0116 236 4325**
Fax: (00 44) **0116 234 0205**